HOOKED

The Secret of Secrets, Book 3

The Final HACK

HOOKED

The Secret of Secrets, Book 2

The Final HACK

ISBN-13: 978-09914589-6-7

Published by Spring Canyon Media
Herriman, Utah

To the secrets I keep close and the friends I keep even closer.

Chapter One

Beyond the secrets we think we know, lie the truths we may not want to.

I boarded the flight from D.C to Anchorage at 4:45 early Friday morning. The sun had yet to rise over the nation's capital but my mind and my heart were aglow. If I'd done my diligence in hunting him, Seth—er Gregory—could be in my company by day's end. If I'd botched my research or made the slightest misjudgment, I could be heading toward trouble.

Settling into the window seat on the last leg of my sixteen-hour travel day, I hoped the first scenario would play out—fireworks, romantic interludes, and all that jazz you see in movies—but I was cautiously prepared for the worst. I'd had the information from Gregory's enlistment papers for less than twenty-four hours, barely long enough to process his identity and book a flight to Alaska. But just because he'd lived in Kenai when he was eighteen didn't mean he was there now.

The flight attendant, a middle-aged brunette with deep crow's-feet and matronly smile, stood at the front of the twelve-passenger plane and called for our attention. I watched the blue sleeves on her arms wave around as she delivered her flight-safety spiel, but I didn't really hear her words. I was too busy rethinking everything I'd learned about Gregory Knight.

I drew a deep breath and anchored my feet to the floor as the flight attendant finished her memorized dialogue and the tiny plane jerked to life. Moments from leaving the gate, the plane went from zero to stretch-the-skin-on-your-face speed across the tarmac. I wrapped my fingers around the armrest, squeezing harder and harder until my knuckles turned white. My nerves— already dancing with anticipation and worry—keyed in to each bump and jitter of the small aircraft. The twists in my stomach shifted from anxiety about what lie ahead to fear about what lie below. I took slow, deliberate breaths and counted down from five.

The flight from Anchorage to Kenai was less than half an hour. Silently assuring myself that I could endure anything for thirty minutes, I directed my focus out the window. Mile after mile of forested land filled my view. Even in the bumpy plane, it was beautiful. Trees dotted the mountain tops like sprinkles on a cupcake and I began to understand why Gregory, or anyone for that matter, might fall in love with this place. But, what if this wasn't the place? What if I'd completely misinterpreted all the information I'd collected? I filled my lungs with the stagnant cabin air and released it again slowly.

Still gripping the armrest, I closed my eyes and pressed my head into the back of the seat. As I reevaluated the data I'd collected for the thousandth time, I overheard the conversation from the passengers behind me. The excited exchange between the two men helped settle the doubt that kept trying to derail me. They were going fishing. I had to be on the right track. Where else could Seth—er, Gregory—have meant with the only piece of information he'd given me? He was going fishing. Kenai was his home town. It was known for fishing. Easy connection. Done, right?

The rush of confidence that had me booking a last minute ticket, calling in sick to work, and throwing all caution to the wind, started to surge back to life. Alaska, the last frontier. Home of great big grizzly bears, record salmon trophies, and hopefully Gregory Knight.

By the time my plane touched down at the Kenai Municipal Airport, the better part of the day was gone. But even sixteen hours of travel—including two layovers, six mini bags of pretzels, and an overpriced, under satisfactory sandwich between gates in Denver— wasn't enough to exhaust my spirit. I was a girl on a mission. A mission to find the man who'd stolen my heart.

STEPHANIE CONNELLEY WORLTON

Chapter Two

What finding Greg actually meant, I still didn't know. Maybe his secrets were too big for me to handle. Maybe my life would be better off without him. And maybe it wouldn't. Either way, I was determined to find him.

Hopefully, I hadn't wasted a full day and two week's salary for nothing.

I grabbed my backpack from the overhead bin and followed the small group of passengers off the plane. I was one of two females on the flight and probably the only traveler not wearing flannel and toting some kind of fishing gear. I smiled down at my Yoda T-shirt, proud of my inner-geek. In the terminal, I slipped around the luggage carousel, happy that I'd fit everything I needed for my short stay in my backpack, and pulled out my cell phone. Switching it off of airplane mode, the service icons came to life. Two texts from David Carey, my co-worker, neighbor, and sort-of-friend buzzed through.

6:30 am: Hey, Kravitsch told me you called in sick today. I hope everything is okay.

2:14 pm: I stopped by your house and interestingly enough, you don't seem to be there. I hope you didn't do something stupid.

Yeah, me too.

Doing the time conversion in my head, I determined that David's texts had been the bookends to his work day. I stared at the screen until the messages faded to black. According to the clock on my phone, it was nearly 8:00 pm Alaska time. That meant it was close to midnight in Maryland. Being a Friday night, I was sure David was settled into his folding chair, staring intently at his computer monitor, and trying to conquer some digitally rendered foe. Should I reply back to him? The memory of his face when he realized I was in love with the man he'd so diligently helped me hunt, was fresh in my mind. His naturally buggy eyes had rounded out behind his glasses, growing bigger than I ever imagined possible, before drooping to the ground. I'd interpreted the somber retreat as an indication that he'd developed an interest in me. The feeling wasn't mutual, nor ever would be. We were too much alike. Two introverts trying to survive in an extroverted world had no business being more to each other than friends.

I decided not to text him back—at least not immediately. I could reply later. For now, I had other things on my mind.

Like food. And transportation. And Mr. Make-my-knees-buckle Gregory Knight.

My backpack fit loosely over my shoulder as I exited the terminal and made my way across the street to the car rental facility. The wind cut through my T-shirt and, had I had to walk another fifty-feet, I would've stopped to dig a jacket out of my backpack. It was Alaska in late August, for heaven's sake, I knew it would be colder than home. My brain had anticipated the chill, but my body was still expecting summer.

Shivering, I rushed into the small car rental office and let the door slam behind me.

"Can I help you ma'am?" The man looked to be the same age as my father, but it was hard to tell under his Grizzly-Adam's beard and tattered baseball cap. His blue flannel shirt was tucked into his jeans, highlighting both his round belly and the large, gold and silver belt buckle that held his pants up.

"Yes," I offered. "I'd like to rent a car, please."

"Great. What's your reservation number?" His untamed mustache danced over his upper lip.

"Oh, well"—I stood confidently in front of his counter. "I don't have one. This was kind of a last minute thing," I began to explain. "Whatever you've got will be great. I'm not picky."

The bush over his lip tweaked up at its corner. I think he was smiling but the words that came out of his mouth were anything but humorous. "I'm sorry ma'am, but we're all booked up for the weekend. It is a holiday you know. Lots of folks have Monday off."

"Oh," I answered, analyzing my new setback. There weren't many social skills I considered myself to be good at. Gratefully, thinking on my feet was one of them. "Is there some other rental facility nearby that you can direct me to?"

He keyed something into his computer then looked up at me. "Looks like one of our competitors has a passenger van available."

"Great." I asserted with as much confidence as I could muster. I had no need for such a large vehicle, but I'd take whatever I could get. "I'll take it. What's their contact number?" I pulled out my phone and waited to key the information in.

"It's in Anchorage," he answered.

I looked up in time to catch a full set of white teeth smile from under the shag of his facial carpet.

"You're kidding, right?"

"Nope."

I tapped my finger nervously on the counter. "Okay, then"—I shook off the disappointment. "I suppose I can always use Uber."

"Not sure how well that'll work for you up here, ma'am. But, if you're interested, I called a taxi for you."

He pointed a long sausage finger toward the curb in front of the shop. A white SUV with a taxi sticker on the side was just pulling to a stop. "I hope you enjoy your stay."

"Thanks." Renewed in my commitment to remain optimistic, I pulled my jacket out of my bag, slid it over my shoulders, and stepped outside to the awaiting cab.

"Welcome to Kenai," the cabby, an older gentleman with a thick pile of silver hair and skin as pale as an arctic winter, greeted me as he held the SUV door open. "Is this your first time visiting us?"

"Yes," I answered, grateful that the hiccup in my transportation plan had at least found resolution with a kind, gentlemanly taxi driver. I slipped the backpack off my shoulder, tossed it onto the seat, then climbed in beside it.

I took a quick inventory of the SUV. The black leather seats were definitely worn, but it was clean and smelled of fresh pine. There was a third row of seats behind me and plenty of elbow room across the middle bench where I sat. Definitely more vehicle than required for a single passenger, but it was better than walking.

The wind whipped through the car as the driver opened his door and hopped into his seat. "Whew!" He shook his head and reached for his seat belt. He had a paternal softness about him that reminded me of my grandfather. Gray curls framed his leathered face then settled over the collar of his shirt. "Once that sun starts to set, the temperature sure does drop."

I peeked up toward the instrument panel. A thermostat indicator sat directly under the cabby's nameplate. The engraved aluminum badge identified my driver as George, the outside temperature was forty-seven degrees Fahrenheit—a full thirty degrees cooler than the weather I'd left in Maryland—and the internal temperature of the vehicle was sixty-eight degrees. I catalogued the three random pieces of information into my memory, unsure how any of them would be of value ever again, but—like most data I collected—I was unable to toss them aside.

"Where to?" George smiled at me through his rear-view mirror.

"Do you know of a place by the name of Gone Fishin'?" I asked, assuming everyone in a city of less than 8,000 residents should be pretty familiar with every other person and establishment in town.

"Sure," he nodded. He put the car in drive and pulled onto the road without further invitation for conversation.

Settling in for what I hoped would be a quiet ride, I awed at the rich luster of greenery out every window of the cab. The setting sun painted brilliant reds and oranges on the horizon, casting long shadows through the dense pine trees.

The road stretched on for miles of what felt like uninhabited forest land, though an occasional street light or business sign indicated some population must exist. Twenty-five minutes passed before the cab slowed and made a turn off the main road. Gravel grated under the tires, pinging in soft reverberations off the undercarriage of the SUV. My heart began to pound fiercely at the wall of my chest. The moment was at hand. I was about to meet my destiny… whatever that might be.

David's warning jumped into my mind. "Not only is he capable of killing someone, Samantha, he's trained to do it." I tried to shake his worry, but as my target got closer and closer, I gave the words credence. David had told me to drop my obsession and my hunt, but I hadn't listened. What if he'd been right? What if Gregory really was dangerous?

As a cautionary measure, and perhaps even a mocking one, I pulled out my phone and sent a text off to David. "I've arrived safely in Alaska. I left your laptop on my kitchen table. If you don't hear from me again by Sunday, you can assume you were right."

I chuckled at my own cryptic message. David's paranoia had gotten almost comical. Even if Gregory wasn't destined to be the love of my life, he most certainly wasn't a threat to it.

The SUV came to stop in front of a large log cabin. "This is it," George announced.

I reached for the door handle then, looking out the window at the log columned entry and two-story elevation, paused. "Are you sure?" I asked. "This doesn't look like the pictures I saw on the web."

"Gone Fishin' Lodge," he stated as he pointed at the painted sign above the door.

"But"—I questioned both my research and my memory. "I think I was expecting a little fishing cabin, not a full lodge with accommodations and such."

The cabby rested his hand on the shoulder of the passenger seat as he turned around to look at me. The wrinkles that encased his eyes were soft, but as he scrunched his forehead in thought, they gave him a wise and pensive appearance. "You mean, like a little log shack with a tiny porch and grumpy old lab standing guard?"

"Well, I'm not sure about the grumpy old dog, but the rest sounds about right. They do fishing tours. Just a small place, I think. Do you know it?"

A quick grin floated across his face. "I think you may be talking about Kristin Knight's little fishing gig."

"Yes!" I perked up at the mention of the Knight name. "I guess I should've been more specific when I told you the name of the place. I didn't realize Kenai was big enough to have two companies with very similar names."

"No, no," he said. "It's my fault. This here lodge is technically in Soldotna, not Kenai. The other fishing and charter company is in Kenai. I assumed you were looking for somewhere to settle in for the night, not a fishing tour." He shook his head and offered an apologetic grin. "No offense, but you don't look like a girl who dressed to go fishing."

He was right. Though I hadn't felt overdressed when I boarded the plane in Maryland, my themed T-shirt and demi-designer jeans felt a little out of place in the outskirts of Alaska.

He turned back around, powered off the taxi's meter, then put the SUV into drive. "My mistake. Let me take you to right place. No charge."

We backtracked through the forested road, then crossed over the Kenai River and wound our way through the markings of the small town of Soldotna. I appreciated George's quiet manner—I was a girl who loved to keep to herself—but he'd mentioned the Knight name as if he knew the family and I couldn't help but wonder how.

"Do you know the Knight family very well?" I asked.

"Not really. Kristin was friends with my daughter in high school. She was a good kid. They had a lot of fun together." He kept his eyes on the road and I thought he was done, then he smiled and added, "That was a long time ago."

"Thirty years, I'd imagine."

He pondered the comment for a minute. "Close. Twenty-eight. Way before you were born." The orange hues of the setting sun set his cheeks aglow as he smiled.

I did the math in my head. If Kristin graduated twenty-eight years ago, then she was now about fifty-six. And, I considered Gregory's age, she must have married and had him shortly after high school. Interesting fact, but really, not important to my mission.

"Can I ask how you know her?" George turned the

car off the highway and headed back west down a two-lane road.

"I don't, really. I'm a friend of her son's." The words popped out of my mouth without much thought. If Gregory had gone through so much trouble to hide his identity, was it wise to divulge any information I might have? But—I considered the situation—I wasn't really divulging information, not anything anyone who'd lived in Kenai wouldn't have known anyway. It was a small town. I couldn't imagine that Kristin had kept Gregory hidden under a rock for his whole life. I took comfort that the comradery of a small town is probably what had made it so easy for him to hide in plain sight, even if I still didn't understand why he was hiding in the first place.

"I can't say I really know her kids," George shrugged. "I moved away shortly after my daughter graduated. Decided to come back when I retired from the railroad last year."

I nodded as if he could see me then, deciding he probably didn't have any information of value to my mission, looked out the side window. Daylight was disappearing at about the same rate as my hope of completing my mission by day's end. I'd wanted to connect with Gregory—hug him, kiss him, hold him—before the day was over.

Based on the sun's position on the horizon, I calculated that I had about twenty minutes before the deep thicketed forests were dark. Suddenly I was grateful for George's company. My nerves were enough of a wreck as it was, I didn't need to be driving around the unfamiliar streets of a sparsely populated, dirt road and no-services area on my own.

In a strange deja vu, George turned the car down a stretch of gravel road. Heavily wooded on both sides, there wasn't much to see other than tree after tree after tree. Gravel kicked and spit on the underside of the carriage, just like it'd done before, and an eerie sense of familiarity came over me. He could've taken me right back to the same location we'd just left and I wouldn't have been the wiser. Or worse. Maybe I'd put too much trust in him all together. Maybe he was a serial killer or a rapist.

I stared up at him through the corner of my eye. He might have been older than me, but even my youth couldn't hold up against a guy twice my size. He could drag me off into the forest and nobody would ever find me.

I sent David another quick text. It simply contained two words: Kenai, Alaska.

Moments that seemed like ages dragged out while George navigated down the conifer walled road. It really couldn't have been more than a minute or two, but as I anxiously awaited to emerge from the thicket, time warped to a near stop. When the forest finally opened up to a shoreline, I felt the air refill my chest.

Nestled between a stand of aspens and a straggly pine tree, stood a wooden sign with the words "Gone

Fishin' Tours and Charters" carved into it. And just beyond that, sat the small fishing cabin I'd seen on the internet.

My heart rushed with anticipation. I'd found it! Gregory's family business was more than just a digital image in cyber space. It was real. Which meant he had to be real, too, right?

I stared out the window at the cabin, the buzz in my chest raging.

"Doesn't look like anyone's here," George cut into my silent celebration. "I'm guessing we probably just missed 'em." He tucked his lips in with a look of guilt. "I'm sorry. It's my fault. If I hadn't gone to the wrong place, you might have been here in time to catch someone."

I opened the door and stepped out into the twilight. The sting of the cold evening coupled with the pang of near success, caused me to shiver. I folded my arms across my chest and, rubbing my hands over my arms, drew a deep breath.

"Go ahead," George rolled down his window to speak to me. "Walk around for a minute. Maybe someone is here. I'll wait for you." He winked in a way that made me feel embarrassed that I'd conjured thoughts about him being a serial killer. I needed to tuck my paranoia away and quit acting like a pansy. I had a mission to accomplish and being a baby wasn't going to get it done.

"Are you sure?" I asked.

"Yup. No hurry. Do what you need to do."

I tucked my hands in my jacket pocket and walked slowly toward the cabin's front steps. Even before I saw the "Closed" sign hanging in the window, I knew George was right. There wasn't a single car in the dirt parking lot and I couldn't imagine any houses were close enough that somebody would've walked here.

"Just my luck," I mumbled as I peeked through the window at the small bait and tackle shop inside. Framed photos of fishermen with their prized catches covered the walls. Many of them were yellowed with age, but a few of them looked new. A large photo above the cash register caught my eye. In it stood a man and a woman, each kissing a sizeable fish on the mouth. The thought made me want to gag.

I jerked my eyes to the picture beside it. A large man, blonde and fit, filled the frame. Even through the glass I could feel the power of his bright blue eyes. A warmth flowed over me. I knew those eyes—well, not those exact ones, per say, because the man in the photo was clearly older than my Seth. But, it was undeniable. The family resemblance didn't lie. There was no doubt that I was in the right place.

CHAPTER THREE

"Can you take me one more place?" I hopped into the back seat, determination renewed. Gregory was near. I could feel it.

"If there's one thing I know, it's that you don't tell a woman no to anything." He turned the key and started the car. "Where to next, sweetie?"

"Do you know where Kristin Knight lives?" I asked hopefully.

"Sorry." He shrugged. "Can't say that I do."

I pulled out my phone and recited the address I'd pinned in my notes. "Sorry," I said, noticing that he wasn't plugging it into his navigation system. "Do you need me to repeat that so you can plug it in?"

"Not necessary," he answered. "I may not keep up on the townsfolk or the small-town rumor mill, but I am quite familiar with the layout of the land. That street is just up around the corner a mile or so. I'm sure I can find it."

"Okay." I nestled back in the seat and began dreaming up fantasies about my reunion with Seth—ugh, Gregory.

Gregory. Gregory. Gregory. I repeated his name over and over in my head. For months he'd been Seth, how was I supposed to all of a sudden call him a new name?

I didn't have much time to build a plan or burn Gregory's name on my lips before George was pulling the car to a stop. "It's that place right there." He pointed out the driver's side window at a red brick rambler on the opposite side of the street.

I zipped my jacket up tight to my chin and reached, with a shaking hand, for the door handle. "Third time's the charm, right?" My voice quivered with a combination of nerves and excitement.

"Can I ask you something?" George twisted in his seat and looked me in the eye. "What exactly are you looking for?"

I returned his look but didn't answer immediately. We were relative strangers, what made him think I was after something in particular? And, more so, what made him think he had the right to ask?

"I don't mean to pry," he started again, "but I've seen that fire in a girl's eyes before. A man never forgets *that* look. Vigor. Determination. Hunger."

Hunger. The growl in my stomach reminded me

that I still hadn't addressed that issue. But, he was right. The drive that propelled me was greater than any emptiness in my gut. I was hungry—ravenous even—to feel Gregory's warmth and hear him say those three most precious words to me again.

I felt my face blush. "Is it that obvious?"

George simply nodded.

I took three deep, purposeful breaths as I calculated an answer. "This isn't my normal modus operandi, just so you know. I'm not one of those crazy, psycho stalker girls." That was the understatement of the year. I was responsible, thoughtful, and very deliberate in everything I did. Except when it came to Gregory. What had gotten into me?

George probably thought I was a total nut job. I worried that he was right.

"What do I owe you?" I said, not wanting to deal with the psychology of why—or how—this stupid love thing had turned me into a different person.

"Nothing."

"That's kind of you," I said as I pulled my wallet out of the front pocket of my backpack, "but I've taken over an hour of your time, plus heaven knows how much gas. Let me at least top off your tank."

As I reached over the console to set a small bundle of cash on his dash, the sound of moving tires rumbled up the gravel road. A green Jeep passed by the driver's side of our SUV then turned into the driveway of Kristin Knight's house. Both George and I forgot about the money and watched intently as the Jeep pulled to a stop.

Time stopped as the Jeep's door swung open and a set of booted feet swung out of the cab. The boots hit the dirt driveway with a thud, stirring up a small dust cloud. But it wasn't the boots or the dust that halted my breath. It was the man who'd graced my dreams for more nights than I could count.

Paralyzed by the reality of his presence, I watched intently as Gregory closed the driver's door. He zipped the front of his jacket up then walked around to the passenger side of the SUV and opened the rear side door. Elation washed over me as I watched him through the tint on my window. He looked every inch the Greek Adonis that'd filled my time in Utah with such purpose and belonging. His blonde hair was a bit longer than the last time I'd seen him and his jawline reflected the shadow of a beard, but both changes looked good on him. Even in his flannel jacket and work boots, he looked runway ready. I imagined myself folding into his strong arms. He'd pull me into his chiseled chest, then tenderly kiss my lips, then…

"Is that him?" George whispered into the silence, breaking my daydream.

My voice croaked out a squeaky, "Yes."

"Well, what are you waiting for? Go get your man."

I settled my hand on the door handle and slowly pulled it open. My feet hadn't even hit the ground when I realized what Gregory had gone to the other side of his car to retrieve. The processing sensors in my mind went into overdrive. Could it? No… How?

A child. A young child.

From my perch behind the taxi door, I watched as he hoisted the blond haired, wide-eyed boy into his arms. The two giggled in unison then Gregory kissed the boy's round cheek and set him down. The kid's little feet sprang into action the second they hit the ground, carrying him across the lawn and toward the house. The front door swung open and a beautiful golden-haired woman emerged from it. She was tall and fit and nearly flawless as she exchanged smiles with Gregory and then the giggly boy. The child ran directly to her, nearly jumping into her arms as she scooped him off the ground and planted her lips on his cheek.

I didn't wait around to see the rest of the exchange.

"Get me out of here!" I demanded as I leapt back into the taxi. Tears escaped my eyes as I slammed the door closed.

"Where would"—George started.

"Anywhere." I cut him off. "Or nowhere. I don't care. Just not here."

George, obliging my request, flipped a U-turn across the gravel road and sped away.

Less than an hour in Alaska and I was done. Game over.

CHAPTER FOUR

The steel guitar of a country ballad assaulted my ears as I pushed the heavy wood door open and stepped inside. Bart's Outrigger Tavern—more of an old saloon than a twenty-first century bar—sat on the corner lot of the hotel I'd had George drop me off at. Drinking wasn't something I typically did—as in, I'd never actually done it before—but after the day I'd had, I thought a shot of something to help dull my senses was well in order.

My chest pounded frantically as I clenched my jaw and tried to ignore the rollercoaster of emotions brewing inside my chest. I couldn't decide if I was more upset at the realization that Gregory Knight had played me for a fool or the fact that I had allowed myself to get swept away by my feelings.

I let my eyes adjust to the dim lighting then stepped

up to the bar. I should've done more homework. I should've dug deeper and not been so quick to follow my heart. If I'd have stuck to the data and dug until I couldn't have dug any deeper, I wouldn't have rushed through my emotions and got on that stupid plane.

"What are you having?" the bartender asked, seemingly flexing his biceps as he spoke. His tatted arms, gaged ears, and artistically groomed facial hair made him arguably the most metro person I'd seen in over twenty-four hours.

"Umm," I stalled. Even in college I'd never had the desire to drink. I glanced behind the bar at the colorful collection of bottles then down the line at the other patron's beverages. "Whiskey," I ordered with feigned confidence. "On the rocks."

A short, balding man noticeably sized up my scrawny legs and less-than-ample chest before offering me the bar stool beside him. A day of travel and heartbreak couldn't have possibly looked good on me. My red hair had started the day pulled back in a somewhat decent ponytail. Many hours and miles separated me from that reality. Throughout the day, small twists and curls had escaped from the hairband, leaving the run-away strands to tickle and annoy my cheeks like little gypsies in a circus. And my makeup—whatever had survived the long trip—had certainly been cried off during the cab ride to the hotel. I probably should've stepped into the restroom and pulled myself together, but I didn't care. If dark streaks of mascara wanted to paint their way over my otherwise naked cheekbones, more power to them.

And if a man wanted to check me out… I didn't finish the thought before turning my back to him. Ignoring his presence was easier than trying to acknowledge his drunken come-ons or lack of judgement. I didn't want him to buy my drink. I didn't want to dance. And I most certainly didn't want to talk. All I wanted was a dark, lonely corner where I could wallow away in self-pity.

Picking up my newly poured beverage, I scanned the establishment for an empty table. Smoke billowed from the side of the room closest to the live band. I decided against sitting in the heart of a smoke cloud and instead filed through the sea of flannel and cowboy boots to an empty corner booth on the opposite side of the small building.

As I slid into the booth, the cowboy band finished up a song about huntin' and fishin' and opened into a twangy ballad about unrequited love. The irony wasn't lost on me. I had Todd—a desirable, heart-throb musician, by all accounts—who wasn't afraid to let me know how hard he was willing to work for me. He was hot and determined and even my own dad loved him. And where was I? In a smoky, testosterone-filled, Alaskan tavern, pining over a different man. An unattainable man. A man who'd built a life on secrets and lies.

I stared at the amber colored drink in front of me.

Three large ice cubes sat heavily on the bottom of the glass, filling most of the space, as sweat beads formed around the perimeter. How had I gotten myself into this mess?

Four-thousand miles away, on the eastern coast of the U.S., groupies were throwing themselves at a man who wanted me. Me. Not a beautiful, golden-haired, Alaskan girl. Just me. Plain old, socially-awkward, crazy, red-headed me.

Pulling the untouched glass closer to me, I dragged my finger through the sweat trail it left across the table. I'd screwed up. Big time. And not just about Alaska. I'd let false confidence override my rational senses. I'd let the fairytale of Gregory overshadow the reality of Todd.

As the band kicked up another song, I imagined the girls undoubtedly flocking to Todd's stage. He was likely just finishing up his final set for the night and I was sure the flattering words and indiscrete propositions were already floating his way. Maybe tonight would be the night he would take their intoxicated bait. Maybe, I winced at the thought, he already had.

My heart sank even deeper.

Each song the band played only drove home the depth of my stupidity. I'd checked marriage records, but how had I been so naïve as to believe that Gregory was a traditionalist? People didn't necessarily get married these days. Families were created left and right without legal documentation. I should've at least considered the possibility.

Tracing my finger over the rim of the whiskey glass, I recalled the boy. Even from a distance, his thick blonde hair and round eyes bore more than an uncanny resemblance to Gregory's. He couldn't deny a connection to the boy if he tried. I had no intention of asking him to. I also had no intention of trying to compete with a beautiful, long-legged blonde.

I pulled George's business card out of my pocket and stared at the number. Maybe if he could take me to the airport first thing in the morning I could get a standby ticket to Anchorage and then figure out my way home.

"I hadn't pegged you as a drinker." A tall, slender silhouette filled my left peripheral.

"I think you've mistaken me for someone else." I turned toward the woman.

Dark, slim jeans tightly hugged her long, thin legs. I followed the horizontal lines of her blue and white striped shirt upward, climbing them with my eyes like they were a ladder. Each line that took me closer to her face, was fitted to her delicate torso. The blouse framed every inch of her fit body perfectly, as if it'd been custom made for her subtle curves. Long, golden hair flowed well below her shoulder line, framing her neck and face. Her eyes met mine and recognition flooded over me.

"I'd rather be alone if you don't mind." I shifted my gaze back down to the little paper card in my hands.

She slid onto the bench across from me and smiled

graciously. "You know, you picked the one place in town that Greg can't come."

Observing the sweat formations on my untouched glass, I purposefully avoided looking at her. "I must have missed the sign restricting his patronization."

Why was she here? Why was she talking to me? Shouldn't she be home basking in the warmth of her beautiful little family?

Unfazed by my snarky quip, the pretty blonde continued. "Greg told me you were a master hacker so I can only conclude one of two things: either you're genuine in your ignorance about Bart's or you came here specifically to avoid Greg."

"I don't know who you think I am, but I have no idea what you're talking about."

"Samantha, right?"

He'd talked about me? To *her*? I simply raised my brows.

"I assumed of all the facts you might find on Greg," she continued, "his connection to Bart's Outrigger Tavern would've been a fairly easy one."

"You know what they say about assumptions." I didn't feel like playing nice. I was irked. What had he told her about me? Did she know that he'd kissed me? Or held me? Or told me that he loved me? Doubtful. He wasn't just a liar; he was a master liar. The king of deceit. And here she was, ready to rub her happy-ever-after in my face. If she only knew the truth . . .

"If you don't already know the details, then they're

not mine to share." She waved down the waitress. "Can I get a number seven, please?"

"Sure thing, sweetie."

The waitress walked toward the bar and disappeared into the back before I pushed out the words formulating in my mind. "So you came to tell me that you can't tell me anything? That was very kind of you." I didn't even pretend to smile. I felt sorry for her. Sorry for me. How many other girls had he tangled in his net?

"No." She shook her head and grinned. "I came to tell you that whatever you think you saw this evening, wasn't what I think you think it was."

"And what exactly is it that you think I thought I saw?"

"I'd imagine you saw Greg with Clay and jumped to some sort of conclusion." She scooted forward on the bench and extended her hand across the table toward me. "I'm Jacey."

Ignoring her gesture, I knotted my hands together and tucked them tightly between my thighs. "Jacey Knight?" I recognized the name from the census records I'd pulled. As per the last record Jacey lived in a house with KJ and Gregory Knight.

"Yes." Her eyes twinkled as if they held some deep dark secret. She radiated a confidence I'd have admired had I not felt so sorry for her. Greg had lied to her more than he'd lied to me. He'd dragged her along for years—three at least, based on the kid.

"Why are you here?" I scowled the words, leaving

her out-stretched hand untouched. I was still trying to figure out why Greg's wife—or girlfriend, or whatever label they'd slapped upon themselves—had taken it upon herself to track me down. If I had the option of holding Gregory or staring down a stranger in a smoky tavern, I certainly know which one I'd choose.

"Because I love my brother."

I rubbed my forehead, trying to process her words. "Your brother?"

"Yes." She grinned as if she finally realized the source of my indignation toward her. "Greg is my brother."

Suddenly the likeness became almost uncanny. The blond hair, the azure blue eyes, the golden skin. The gently curved lips.

I bowed my head, ashamed that I'd allowed my insecurities to take control. Chastising myself, I took a deep breath and let out a little chuckle. It seemed I was creating quite the habit of overlooking important things and jumping to premature conclusions, but this . . . well, this was a new low. I wasn't the other woman. And neither was she.

"And the kid?" I asked.

"Clayton is my entire life. He's my son."

My chest lightened as relief flooded over me. "So…" I took a deep, thoughtful breath. "Greg doesn't have a kid?" Not that that would matter. A kid was one thing, many men my age had them, but a man in a relationship was another. I was a lot of stupid things, but a homewrecker wasn't one of them.

The azure tint of her perfectly round eyes softened as her rose colored lips turned up into a grin. "Not that I'm aware of."

"And he's not involved in a relationship?" My spirit lifted. The validity of my spontaneous trip hung on Jacey's answer.

Loose blonde curls danced over her shoulders as she shook her head. "No."

The tension in my chest and shoulders instantly abated. I unclenched my hands and settled them on my lap. My spontaneous acts hadn't been misguided. I hadn't overlooked something. I still had a chance with Gregory. I let out a sigh of relief.

"But," she leaned forward and spoke softly across the table. "I should warn you that he has a past that weighs heavily on his present. Any thoughts you have of building something with my brother ought not to be taken lightly."

"What's that supposed to mean?" Maybe I'd jumped too quickly in giving myself hope. Or, maybe his sister was a little too overprotective.

"You are aware of his military background, correct?"

"Yes." Kind of. The U.S. Military didn't have records of Gregory Knight or any of his multiple aliases in their general files. I'd had to hack into the dark parameters of the government's internal, non-existent, darknet to gain any sort of trail on him. But even then, the records weren't complete. Some details had been deliberately deleted and deeply hidden. No one, not me nor my brilliant hacking friend David, could access them.

"And you know that he is no longer active in the Navy, right?"

"Yes." I nodded my answer.

"And you're aware of his court-martial?" She continued to lean across the table, her eyes intently focused on mine.

Negative. I shook my head.

"Well that explains why you don't know about his non-patronage of Bart's." Her eyes bounced around the bar as if it was an important key to Greg's past.

I was more than confused. "He was court-martialed and somehow that has something to do with the bar?" It wasn't the real question on my mind. No, that one sounded more like a screaming siren. Why had he undergone a court-martial? And did it have anything to do with why his military records had disappeared?

"I'm sorry, I wish I could tell you what you want to know, but Greg's secrets are his to tell, not mine."

I could respect that. I should respect that. But why did the man have to have so many secrets?

The waitress reappeared with two glasses of water and a basket full of chicken fingers and fries. Jacey thanked her then picked up a fry.

"If he can't come here, can you take me to him?" I asked as she took a small bite off the top of the steaming hot potato slice. There was no time like the present.

"No." She looked down at the watch on her wrist. "I don't think that'd be a good idea. It's nearly midnight and he's got an early morning and a long day ahead of him." She shrugged. "If you want to talk to him, I suggest you wait until tomorrow."

My lip quivered. Would the man always be at arms distance away? I didn't want to be sensible. And I most definitely didn't want to wait another day to see him.

"Please?" I pleaded. I'd come four-thousand miles to talk to Greg and I wasn't going to sleep until I got the chance. I had to believe he wanted to see me, too. If not, why had he invited me to find him?

"Listen, Samantha." She crossed her arms definitively across her chest. "He doesn't know you're here and he most definitely doesn't know that I'm talking to you."

"How is that possible?" I wondered out loud. "He had to have seen the taxi. And what about me? If he didn't see me, then how did you know who I was?"

"I told him the taxi was lost and had stopped for directions." She raised her shoulders. "And you? Well, you ducked back behind the tinted windows so fast he didn't get a chance to see your face." She took a sip of her water. "He has a photo of you on his phone from Utah. Of course, you had brown hair then, and it was a touch shorter, but I still knew it was you."

I ran my fingers over the red locks of my ponytail, grateful it'd grown out a little more in the last month, but more intrigued by the fact that Gregory hadn't tossed me aside as soon as he got home. He'd talked about me and even shared my photo with his sister. The thought gave me confidence.

Jacey continued, "He leaves with a tour at five o'clock in the morning. But —" she pushed my untouched whiskey glass to the side of the table and slid her basket of food in front of me— "he'll be back to shore for a bit in the afternoon. If you want to be to the shop around two, I'm sure he'll be able to break away and talk to you."

Though the thought of waiting until two in the afternoon didn't intrigue me, I agreed quickly and easily. "Okay. Thank you." As the words filtered over my lips, alternate plans began to formulate in my mind. I'd do whatever it took to complete my mission, even if that meant crashing Gregory's fishing party and boarding a fishing boat at the crack of dawn. I didn't just *want* to see him with every fiber of my being, I *needed* to. And I was limited on time.

"Great." Jacey smiled more warmly than she should've. I hadn't exactly welcomed her with open arms or kindness. "The dock is about a half a mile down that dirt road on the other side of the hotel. Do you need me to find you a ride?"

Remembering George's card, I picked it up and tapped it on the table. "I think I can get there. But thank you for the offer."

Zipping her jacket up, she stood and offered one

last smile. "Those are for you." She pointed to the chicken and fries as she dropped a twenty-dollar bill on the table. "I'm guessing you haven't had any real food all day."

CHAPTER FIVE

On the heels of jetlag and a restless night, my four o'clock alarm felt more like an oh-dark-thirty bullhorn. I hit snooze twice then finally rolled off of the lumpy hotel mattress and pulled myself together. Dawn hadn't even cracked before I stepped out of the rustic hotel room and into the crisp morning air.

Before climbing into bed I'd mapped the route from my hotel to Greg's fishing shop. Jacey hadn't been exaggerating when she said it was about a half a mile down the road. Figuring the walk would help wake me up, I pulled a beanie over my ears and set off down the tree lined road.

The cool Alaska morning was dark in a way that I'd never experienced dark before. I zipped my jacket high and tucked my hands in my pockets then rounded the corner, leaving the lights of the hotel behind me. A waxing moon hung low over the horizon, playing peek-a-boo through the tops of the pine trees. Though nearly full, it provided little light through the shadows of the forest.

My shoes crunched across the gravel road as I pulled my phone out of my pocket and turned the flashlight app on. Its soft beam provided a small cone of light directly in front of me, but did nothing to hide the shadows in the trees. If anything, it intensified them.

Each step took me farther from the small civilization of the hotel and seemingly deeper and deeper into the forest. Holding on to the memory of the drive down the road the night before, and the excitement at the man I knew waited less than 800 yards south, I drew a deep breath and rallied my courage.

Trying to calm my scattered nerves, I turned to the mathematical calculations of my journey. Estimating my average step to be just over two feet, I converted the impending yards into steps. Eight-hundred yards was about twenty-four hundred feet. Twenty-four divided by two was twelve-hundred.

Wind danced through the branches of the pines, tickling my paranoias. Anything or anyone could have been hiding in the darkness and I'd have never known until it was too late. With the growing knot in my chest, even twelve-hundred steps sounded undoable. Giving myself the benefit of the doubt, I reassessed my steps and decided they were closer to two and a half feet each. At the bigger gate, it'd take just over nine-hundred steps.

I started counting.

I'd barely gone two hundred steps before the thought of bears silenced my ability to count. *Lions and tigers and bears* repeated through my mind. I shook the familiar chant from my head. There were no lions or tigers in Alaska, just bears. Grizzly bears. Big, fat, mean grizzlies.

My pace quickened. Could I outrun a grizzly? I had no idea. I could run fast, but how fast could a grizzly run? Then it occurred to me that I'd once learned that you're not supposed to run from a bear. But what was it you were supposed to do? Curl up in a ball? Look it in the eye? I dug through the files in my memory, hoping to pull the appropriate information.

Don't run. That's what I'd learned. Don't run. I slowed my pace. Don't look him in the eye. Check. No risk of that happening. Don't panic. Don't scream.

Keep calm.

I tuned my ears into every noise—and non-noise— in the surrounding forest. I was alone in the most terrifying sense of the word. I swallowed the lump in my throat and kicked the rationalization out of my head then took off in a full run.

My feet crunched loudly on the gravel road as I rounded one bend and then another before finally catching a glimpse of the lights on the Gone Fishin' tour shack. I brought my run to a halt and gathered my composure. I focused on slowing my labored breath before approaching the small shack.

A handful of cars, including the Jeep I'd seen Gregory hop out of the night before, were parked in a dirt lot beside the log structure. Whispered voices were coming from the dock side of the building. I checked my watch then rounded the corner of the shack. I was right on time. The tour would be leaving any minute.

I counted six men—four of them old enough to be my grandpa, one about my dad's age, and the fifth one a young twenty-something with a ragged beard and backwards ball cap. I scanned the dock area again, but still didn't see any sign of Gregory.

I made one last visual sweep of the dock and was about to spin around when the weight of a hand settled on my shoulder. My body locked and my breath halted.

"When my alarm went off this morning, I never imagined that it would be ushering in a slice of heaven."

I didn't need to see his face to recognize his voice or his touch. "Seth," I whispered through baited breath. I bit my lower lip then slowly turned around.

"Sam."

The hands of time seemingly stopped as I looked through dusk's heavy shadows and up at the man who'd filled my every thought since the day I'd first met him. The cabin's porch light hung over him like a halo, solidifying the god-like status I'd granted him in my dreams. My lip quivered and a flood of warmth ran from my head, through my shoulders and fingertips, then on to my toes.

"Seth," I whispered again, then realizing my error,

smiled and said, "I mean Greg."

"You can call me Seth if I can call you Ginger." His cobalt eyes penetrated through mine and reached deep into my soul. Though I'd dreamed of this moment—the moment when we'd finally meet again—I'd never dared imagine how it would actually play out.

My breath stilled as I tried to process the surge of emotions raging through me. "I don't care what you call me." The words came out as barely a whisper. My hands trembled as I reached toward him, touching my fingers to the short hairs on his cheeks. They were bristly yet soft. Rugged yet sexy.

I leaned into him, cherishing the cadence of his heart beat as I pressed my face into the firmness of his chest. My heart pulsed in rhythm with his as I wrapped my arms tightly around his torso.

He draped his arms around my shoulders, pulling me closer into him and making all the sleepless nights of hacking and digging seem nominal. Moisture filled my eyes. He was real, I repeated to myself. Real. Jolts of electricity shot through me. I couldn't imagine anything better than him holding me forever.

But he didn't. Not even close. Before I could fully catch my breath, he was pulling out of my embrace. "I really didn't expect for you to be here."

I took another deep draw of his musky cologne, then tilted my head up to look at him. "Did you not think that I could find you?" I asked, confused by the heaviness in his eyes.

He took my hands in his and stared intently into my eyes. "I knew if anyone *could*," he emphasized the word, "it'd be you. I just didn't know if you *would*."

"Why would you think that?"

"Let's be honest, Sam, I have a lot of dark spots in my life."

"None of us are perfect." I stared into his blue eyes, inviting him to tell me more. There was relatively little that I did know about Gregory, other than a handful of random data points I'd hacked and the little nugget that Jacey had revealed just hours before. But in the moment, under the flicker of the fishing cabin's light, there seemed no secret so great that it could change the way I felt.

"I don't know about that," Greg said, releasing my hands from his hold then folding his arms across his chest. "If you did the homework I told you to, I'm sure you've got a few things you'd like to talk about."

"Yes," I nodded, my stomach dancing with a different excitement than it had just moments before. Unanswered questions lingered on every breath that I took.

"I still can't believe you're here." He shook his head.

"Me either." My lip trembled and a tear escaped my eye. This wasn't how I'd imagined our reunion. I thought he'd at least kiss me. Did he not hunger for me the way I'd hungered for him?

He swiped his thumb gently across my cheek,

wiping away my tear. "I know you want to talk," he said, "and I wish I'd had a heads up that you were coming," he sighed. "But those gentlemen over there"—he nodded toward the men waiting on the dock— "came a long way to catch themselves a halibut. If I don't get them out on that vessel soon, dawn's going to come and go and we won't have had a single fish in our net."

"I understand." I longed to touch his chest again, if for no other reason than to solidify the reality that he was an actual tangible being. I settled for another hit of his cologne as it intermingled with the mountain air, intoxicating myself with the memories it conjured, then took a step back.

"Would you like to come with us?" As if sensing the slow sinking of my heart, he brushed my hair off my face and offered an irresistibly crooked grin.

"Is there room? I don't want to be in the way." He may not have kissed me, but he wasn't sending me packing either. At least part of my plan was working out.

He led me across the pebbled walk and onto the dock. "If you can handle a bunch of flannel clad men and a few wet, stinky fish, I'm sure we can make room."

CHAPTER SIX

Thanks to the beanie Greg lent me, my ears hadn't lost all of their feeling, but the chill of the morning air had long since numbed my nose. My knuckles were white as I grasped hold of the boat's metal side rail, a combination of my nerves and the bitter blast of headlong wind that assaulted the bow of the boat.

Maybe I should have mentioned my fear of boats before leaving the dock. It seemed like a logical thing to bring up in a conversation prior to embarking on a fishing expedition. Logic, however, was something I appeared to have left at home.

I gripped the rail fiercely as Greg captained the Ooga Booga Fishy—his thirty-five foot Bertram fishing vessel—down the Kenai River. The boat was large and seemingly stable, but not enough to settle my anxieties. After being stuck on a catamaran during a storm as a child, I had legitimate fears. I didn't like boats and I most certainly didn't like deep waters. But I liked Greg. And if it took getting on a boat to spend time with him . . .

Five. Working through the probabilities of an impending disaster, as if that would calm my nerves, I sucked in a deep breath of the cold mountain morning.

Four. Pushing the air back out of my chest, I reminded myself that the chances of ending up in the cold water were slim to none. The fact provided me little reassurance.

Three. I filled my lungs with another deep, thoughtful breath. One in six-million. Those were the odds. And they were good odds . . . just not good enough.

Two. I closed my eyes and tried to force the fear out of my chest with my breath.

One. In. Long. Deep. Relaxing . . . or not. No matter how hard I tried to reason with myself, it wasn't working. I tightened my grip on the railing and focused on not making myself sick.

The six fishermen and Greg's co-captain were divided between the enclosed cabin and the rear deck of the boat. We'd done quick introductions prior to setting off, but other than Austin, the long haired, backwards ball-capped, co-captain and one of the patrons named Don, I hadn't paid much attention to any of their names. If I had, I'd have stored them for reference, but I'd been too busy doing the psychological gymnastics required to get on a boat.

Greg kept inviting me inside and Don continued to offer me his seat. I could tell he was strong and fit for his age, even so, I didn't feel right taking a seat from a seventy-year-old man—especially one sporting a US Marines Veteran jacket. He'd earned both the seat and my respect. Besides, something about the fresh air— cold as it was—helped me maintain my poise and settle my stomach. Kind of.

After nearly an hour traveling on the Kenai River in the dark, we emerged from the confines of the river's edge into the Cook Inlet. Steam rose off the surface of the water, painting a peaceful fog over the big open pool of water. The sun hadn't risen over the eastern horizon yet, but the darkness had begun its retreat into the heavens. Reds and oranges reflected off low hung stratus clouds, casting a pink hue across the water's surface and dusting a flushed glow on the tips of the snowcapped mountains in the distance. It was beautiful. The kind of scene that adorned travel brochures and calendar insets. I released my grip on the rail and pulled out my phone to snap a photo. My body teetered with the currant, making my balance and my logic unsure. I quickly snapped my shot, shoved my phone back in my pocket, and regained my death-hold on the railing.

I was so involved in appreciating nature's awakening that I barely noticed the boat come to a stop. Greg gathered the attention of his tour group and explained the ins and outs of halibut fishing. I hung back, happy to observe. Each man retrieved a large fishing pole from the storage rack attached to the backside of the cabin then proceeded to thread huge hooks onto the line.

Greg's love for his work radiated as he coached the men through the basics of tying a halibut hook. His face was aglow and his words were laced with experience. I didn't care much about fishing, but Greg's passion made for an enjoyable show.

Don finished tying his hook first. After checking the security of the knots, Austin opened a large cooler and pulled out what at first seemed to be a rubber squid bate. As soon as Don plunged it onto the hook, however, the creature bled and squirmed. I turned my head away, nearly gagging at the sight. The poor squid was alive—or, at least, it had been.

One after another the fisherman baited their hooks and cast their lines into the inlet. When the last one was down, Greg pulled a fishing rod off the rack and carried it to me.

"Here." He smiled like a child eager to share his most prized possession. "This one's for you."

"Oh, no." I shook my head emphatically. "I'm good." I waved my hand in front of me as if casting a spell to keep the rod away.

"Come on," he said. "You can't come all the way to Alaska, get on a boat, and *not* throw a line in the water."

"Oh, I'm going to throw *something* in the water." I grabbed both sides of his collar and gave them a playful tug. Though I knew I didn't have the actual strength to move him, he fell forward, pinning me between the railing and his body. I tightened my hold on his jacket.

"If you're not careful," he raised an accusing brow, "we're both going to end up in the drink."

I wasn't good at witty retorts, especially while trying to combat my fear of the deep. My fingers laced tightly over his collar as I tried to construct some kind of clever comeback. Before I had a chance, though, a wave smacked the side of the boat. We rocked first to the left, then to the right. I lost hold of his collar. My body pitched forward then quickly backward toward the edge of the boat again. In full panic, I lurched toward Greg and threw my arms around his torso.

"You're okay," he said, securing me in his hold. "I promise it would take a lot of effort to fall over that edge."

"If there's a way, I'm sure I'll figure it out." My voice quivered into his chest.

"Then I guess I will have to save you."

I tilted my head upward hoping to catch his eye. I wanted to believe he could be my safe place—not just on the boat, but in daily life. His arms were rested around me, but his attention was elsewhere.

"Hey, Norman," he called toward the rear deck. "I think you've got something on your line."

Greg smiled down at me then released me from his embrace.

I settled onto a bench in the middle of the boat, safely away from the edge of the vessel and fought back the frustration of Greg's seeming lack of excitement about my surprise visit. Strategically distanced from the commotion of the fishing party, I dismissed the disparaging thought, assuring myself that he simply needed to attend to his customers' needs. We'd have our time, I breathed in with conviction. Eventually. I hoped.

Austin and Greg rallied around the fisherman, coaching him in his effort to reel in the fish at the end of his line. I was unimpressed with the process and found myself riveted by Mother Nature's grand show that was enfolding around us.

The sun crested in such quick, smooth orchestration, it was hard not to take awe. A brilliant band of gold peeked around the volcanic mountains and settled on the horizon. Low hanging clouds glowed bright red and even the water burnt in hues of crimson and orange. I snapped a few more pictures on my phone, eager to show them to my parents when I got home.

Home. That was a part of my plan I hadn't thought through. My home was half way across the globe from Greg's. If things worked out between us—if he decided that he needed me as much as I needed him—where would home be? Our home. I smiled at the thought.

The boat rocked harshly, pulling me from my thoughts. Four of the men, including Greg and Austin, were hovered over the edge of the boat in a calm sort of commotion. I don't know when they'd done it, but both Greg and Austin had pulled on a pair of rubber pants with a bib front and straps that hung off their shoulders. Suddenly my jeans—wrinkly as they were—felt like high-fashion. I smoothed my hands over my thighs then settled them on my knees hoping to counterbalance myself against the swaying.

The fisherman's pole curled nearly in half as the tip bent to touch the water. Something about four feet from the stern held the men's attention. I adjusted my position to see what they were looking at. A huge, flat-bellied fish jumped, tugging at the end of the line and rocking our boat with its power.

Greg calmly coached the fisherman to bring the catch in a little closer. I liked watching him work. He was gentle yet sure in his commands.

The man grunted and pulled the wrestling fish as Greg stuck a long handled implement into the water. A faint pinging sound echoed from Greg's hand as he shot a harpoon into the fish's belly. Austin followed by grabbing the creature with a large steel hook. Together, they hoisted the big, ugly fish over the edge and into the boat.

"Nice catch, Norm." His buddy slapped him on the back as Austin dropped the limp fish to the boat's deck.

I drew my feet up onto the bench and wrapped my arms securely around my legs, wanting no part in the fishing game. Greg laughed as he walked past me and into the cabin where he hung the harpoon back on its rack. He reemerged, touching my knee as he walked by, then bent over the fish with a tape measure. "Forty-two inches," he called. "Not bad for our first catch of the day."

CHAPTER SEVEN

I'm not sure if I'd actually fallen asleep or not, but the growl of my empty stomach had me flinching out of my relaxed state. Greg must have heard it too, because before I knew it he was offering me a package of crackers and a banana.

"I probably should've offered you something earlier," he said, settling into the seat beside me. "I don't imagine you had anything to eat this morning."

"Thanks," I said, taking his offering. "I had a protein bar before I left the hotel." I looked at the clock on my phone. That had been nearly four hours ago.

"Well, we're not much for fancy meals around here, but I've got an extra ham and cheese sandwich in the cooler if you'd like it."

I peeled back the banana peel and took a bite. "No, thank you. These will be fantastic." I nodded at the snacks he'd provided.

"If I'd known you were coming, I'd have packed you some real food." He shrugged.

"Seriously, this is good." I leaned my head on his shoulder. "Thanks for taking in a stowaway."

"The pleasure is mine. I'm glad you get to experience a little slice of my life."

I held on to the first few words. Even though he'd been busy doing his fish-stuff, and I barely felt like he knew I was there, he was *pleased* that I was there. Not okay, or bummed, or dispassionate, but pleased. "It is beautiful." I looked across the vast water at the mountains on the horizon.

"I remember coming out here as a kid and staring up at that big clear sky in pure awe."

I nodded in agreement. The heavens seemed to continue on forever. Big. Bright. Beautiful.

"And my dad . . ." He shook his head with a grin. "If there were ever a master storyteller, it'd be him. You wouldn't believe the stories he would weave. When I was nine he had me and my sister convinced that the fish actually lived inside those volcanoes." He pointed across the water to a beautiful high-rising mountain. "He said every night the volcano would have a party and any fish that were naughty got spouted out the top so we could catch them up the next day."

"And you believed him?" I chuckled at the innocence of a child, realizing I knew virtually nothing about his childhood.

"Only until I told my mom the story. She never came right out and called his bluff, but the way she laughed made me know I'd been fooled."

"I think I like your parents already." As the comment slid off my tongue, it occurred to me that the data fragments I had on his family consisted solely of census records. And those only listed KJ, Jacey, and Greg in the house. No father.

"Not going to lie, I think I hit the parent jackpot," he continued energetically despite my awkward comment. "I mean, really, look at this place. Only the best parents in the world would raise their kid here."

He paused for a moment and, staring out across the water, let out a deep sigh. I reached for his hand. He hesitated for a second then wrapped his fingers around mine.

"My dad was incredible," he continued somberly. "He had a passion for life and nature—and fishing—that was unmatched. He started this company as a way to justify fishing every day. Of course, my mom loved him so much she'd have never thought to protest. I don't think she ever planned on running the business by herself, but"—he shrugged— "I guess no one ever plans on losing the love of their life at such a young age."

He continued answering my questions before I ever got a chance to ask them. "Cancer. Ten years ago. I was a junior in high school. I should've stuck around and helped Mom and Jacey run the company, but I wanted so desperately to make my dad proud. He'd been in the navy and my grandpa had been a marine. As much as my family probably needed me, joining the military seemed like the only honorable thing to do."

I nodded as some of the missing pieces started to slide together. "I met Jacey."

He raised a questioning brow at me.

"Last night," I clarified. "At Bart's Tavern. She seemed very nice."

He continued to look surprised. Clearly, she hadn't said anything to him about me.

"Yes, she is nice," he finally said. "And smart. And sassy. And, well, let's be honest, she's a brat."

"Must be a family trait." I finished the last bite of banana then opened up the bag of crackers.

"Maybe that's why I like you. I know how to deal with you. You're in my comfort zone." He patted his hand on my knee, then stood and moved back to the rear of the boat before I could respond.

I popped a cracker in my mouth, savoring the salt on my tongue as I watched Greg offer Don the same coaching he'd given Norman. He liked me. He'd said it. It wasn't the other "L" word I'd been hoping for, but it was something.

The cracker had nearly dissolved in my mouth before I remembered to chew. He liked me. I held on to the words and the hope that eventually—sooner rather than later—he'd show me just how much.

The day began to warm as the sun ascended higher and higher in the sky. I shed my beanie and unzipped my jacket, appreciating the fresh air as it flowed around me. It was peaceful and quiet to a degree I'd never experienced before. I closed my eyes again, absorbing the tranquility.

*   *   *

"I think it's your turn now." Norman's robust voice cut through the silence as his figure cast a shadow across my face. Coffee stained teeth smiled out from under his mustache and pride glowed from behind the glass of his spectacles. It'd been an eventful morning, most of the fisherman had reeled in a catch. Norm had just finished pulling in his second.

"No, thanks," I shook my head. "I'm good right here." I anchored myself to the bench I'd claimed as my safe zone. The only catch I was interested in getting my hands on was the one wearing rubber fishing pants and an unbuttoned wind breaker. Even though he hadn't had time to devote a lot of attention to me, Greg's hotness was hard to ignore. His blue eyes were the color of the surrounding marine and his smile shone brighter than the midday Alaskan sun. His mere presence had a magical way of making me feel safe—even in the midst of the open water on a rocking fishing boat. I wanted him to hold me and kiss me and . . . Sigh. How long would my lips have to be patient?

"You're goin' to break this old man's heart and turn down my lucky pole?" Norman's eyes turned down sadly as he curled his lips dramatically into a frown.

My heart softened to his plea. How do you turn an old man down? "I don't have a license."

"You can use mine," Greg offered.

I couldn't come up with another excuse. "Fine," I said, taking the pole from Norm's outstretched hand. "But only for a little bit."

"Make me proud, darlin'." The old man grinned.

I committed to minimal effort as Greg tied the line and stuffed a squiggly squid on the hook. Following his instructions, I dropped the line into the water, fed it all the way to the bottom, then reeled it in a couple of turns. Satisfied with my accomplishment and the grin on Greg's face, I settled into a small plastic chair and rested the pole across my knees.

The boat rocked rhythmically with the current, hedging lightly from one side to the other, as the minutes dragged quietly by.

As if sensing my boredom, Don and Norman scooted to my side and began sharing stories about their grandchildren and families. Greg paced between me and the other fisherman, keeping an eye on each of the five poles in the water.

Don's animated stories bled together flawlessly. He told me about his wife then moved through his children and then onto his grandchildren. His biggest delight, it seemed, was a granddaughter who had recently had a daughter of her own. He noted the fact by raising his brows at me then glancing over his shoulder at Greg. "Babies are fun," he said in a tone that denoted how ecstatic he was to be a great-grandfather.

Greg's pacing came to a stop behind me and he rested his hands on my shoulders. "Are you ready?" he asked.

I considered the context of the current conversation and about fell out of my chair. Was he asking if I was ready for children? Talk about mixed signals. We'd barely reunited—hadn't even kissed yet, though I anticipated it with every breath I took—and we were going to talk about children?

I thought about the possibility of a family one day. It was such a foreign yet desirable concept. And one I'd definitely reserved for the future. But only a few weeks had passed since I'd about gotten myself killed. I was barely suited to take care of myself, how could I possible take responsibility for someone else?

I swallowed the lump in my throat. "Sure," I answered with measured doubt.

"Then you better get a good hold on that pole." He reached over me, his strong chest pressing into my shoulders and his firm biceps anchoring over my arms as he secured his hands over mine. "You've got a bite."

I flinched forward with a sigh. He wasn't talking about children. He was talking about fish. Fish I could handle. Maybe.

Greg moved to my side as I stood. The tug on the end of my line was strong. I readjusted my grip on the fishing pole and anchored my feet in a gated stance.

"Keep reeling." Greg's even tone didn't match the rush I felt in my chest. "Slow and steady."

It was all I could do to maintain my balance, hold the pole, and turn the reel at the same time. Gratefully Greg understood the limitations of both my size and experience. He anchored his hands beside mine and offered his strength.

"I think it's a big one," I said. I hadn't noticed how labored my breath had become until I'd tried to speak.

"I think you're right." Austin stared over the edge of the boat and out into the water.

It took all of my energy to crank the reel over and over again. Never had I imagined a fish could put up such a fight. Adrenaline rushed through me and for a moment I understood the draw. This is what it was all about. The thrill of the catch. The rush of anticipation. My arms burned as I continued to try to reel in my line.

"Keep going." Greg held the rod tight, preventing me from being pulled into the water. "Almost there."

Perspiration built on the base of my neck and across my brow. As grateful as I'd been when the sun started warming things up, I hadn't expected to sweat. How very feminine.

"Almost here," Austin yelled as he reached over the edge of the boat, harpoon in hand.

Just then the monster surfaced. My arms jerked forward as the fish flopped from side to side. Then, just feet from the edge of the boat, it jumped out of the water. I gasped at both its size and its power. Don wrapped his arms around my waist and anchored me from behind. Greg inched forward on the pole, creeping toward the end of it, but never letting go.

Norman settled his hands on the rod where Greg's had been. I was grateful for the backup.

"I said the pole was lucky. You didn't have to go show all of us up, though." Norman laughed.

After a few more twists and tugs, I heard Austin's harpoon ring out, but the fish kept fighting. A second harpoon shot fired, and again, the fish pulled and tugged with all its might. In a quick succession of movement, Greg released his hold on the rod, pulled a handgun from his waistband, and fired a single shot at the water.

Immediately, the fighting stopped.

"Why did you shoot it?" I asked as Austin and Greg hooked the beast and dragged it into the boat.

"It was either you or the fish," Austin grunted as he set the halibut down on the deck.

I wasn't sure if he was being facetious or rude. Greg clarified before I got the chance to ask. "Halibut are big and brutal," he explained. "They don't call them the killers of the Pacific for nothing."

"Really?" I asked, still unbelieving that a fish—ugly and big as it might be—could be dangerous.

"Yep." Greg pulled out his measuring tape. "Even a

STEPHANIE CONNELLEY WORLTON

small one can break a man's femur. And look at this guy. Sixty-two inches! That's huge. He'd have taken you out without a second thought."

Austin ran into the cabin to check the weight chart. "That's a hundred and twenty-pound bad boy right there. Way to go, Sam! Best catch of the day."

"Could be our best catch of the season." Greg winked at me with a grin.

"I knew that pole was good luck," Norman chortled.

I let the men do all the necessary fish handling, only getting within arm's length for the obligatory photo with my catch. I didn't mind eating fish, but I wasn't about to touch its slimy, scaly body. Especially on a fish that wore both of his eyes on the same side of his head. Ugly. Yuck.

I stepped into the tiny in-cabin restroom to wash my hands. Though I hadn't actually touched the fish, my hands smelled like I had. As I'd fought to reel in that big ugly boy, fishy smelling water had sprayed off the fishing line and onto everything within twelve inches of the reel.

Smashed in the tiny restroom, I tried to imagine how anyone bigger than myself could close the door behind themselves. The facility was nothing more than a small closet with a toilet and a tiny round sink. There wasn't even a mirror, which was probably a good thing. I couldn't imagine how terrible I must look after a rough night's sleep, an unplanned morning sprint, and a wrestling match with a fish that was bigger than me.

Satisfied with their cleanliness, I finished drying my hands, tossed the wet paper towel into the trash, then left the claustrophobic bathroom quarters and settled back onto the bench just outside the boat's cabin. A light skiff of clouds dusted the sky, but not enough to keep the sun from penetrating through. I kicked my feet up on the bench and leaned back, relishing the warmth of the day and the presence of the only man who'd ever made my heart race like I'd just run the Kentucky Derby.

CHAPTER EIGHT

I don't know what had possessed me to think riding on the open bow in the cold morning hours was a good idea, but I was grateful Don and Greg had convinced me otherwise for the return trip. The afternoon sun had warmed things up significantly, even so, the shelter of the boat's cabin provided a welcome refuge from the crisp wind.

"Do you want to drive?" Greg asked from his position behind the wheel.

"Not particularly," I responded from my seat beside Don. Listening to Don's colorful stories helped sooth the anxieties I hadn't been able to stifle.

"Come on," Greg pleaded.

"I'll go in your stead." Don nudged his shoulder

into mine. Though I didn't know how to banter with him, he'd done a good job making me laugh for hours. "But I kind of have a feeling he's more interested in wrapping his arms around you then actually teaching you about boat operation."

I leaned over and loudly whispered to Don. "Do you think so? I'm not so sure. I think that man loves fish more than women."

"Burn!" Austin stepped out of the cabin restroom just in time to catch my comment. Don and his buddies laughed irreverently.

"That sounds like a challenge, Captain," Don said, pushing me forward.

"Challenge accepted." Greg smiled.

I gripped on to the edge of the cushion, playing along as Don tried to nudge me off my seat. My fingers, however, couldn't maintain grip on the weathered vinyl and I soon found myself slipping onto my feet.

"Fine," I playfully growled, first at Greg then over my shoulder at Don. "But if I sink this vessel and you all find yourselves floating about in that ice cold water, it was not my fault."

"Like I said"—Greg winked at Don— "challenge accepted."

Settling his hand on the small of my back, Greg guided me toward the steering wheel.

"Seriously," I said, appreciating his long-awaited attention, but dragging my feet at the idea of captaining a vessel. "I'm really okay back there hibernating on the bench."

"And like Don said, maybe I just want an excuse to be close to a pretty girl." He situated himself behind me, stretching his arms around my shoulders so he could settle his hands on the wheel next to mine.

My heart leapt. It'd taken the better part of the day, but at last he was done enough with the demands of his job that he could acknowledge me.

He rested his chin over my shoulder and his breath tickled across my cheek. A trail of tingles shot through my neck, starting a chain reaction through my body. "You really are going to make me sink this thing if you keep that up."

"Nah. The Ooga Booga is virtually unsinkable." He offered the words with such confidence my anxieties took a small degree of comfort. His breath dusted over my cheek again, sending another ripple of tingles through me.

This was *my Seth*. The one whose mere presence filled me with warmth and love. The one who made my heart flutter with uncontrollable excitement. The one who'd made me throw caution to the wind and book a trip to the great-unknown.

I wanted nothing more than to turn around and plant my lips on his. But I couldn't. Not while the boat was moving—and especially not while I was at the wheel. The motion, coupled with the anxious knot in my gut, were nothing short of a disaster waiting to happen. If I got sick, all bets were off. No man in his right mind wanted to kiss a girl with puke breath.

I gripped the wheel tightly and took a deep breath.

"The front of the boat is called the bow," Greg said, resuming his role of Captain though I held the wheel. "The back is called the stern."

I was less interested in his boat terminology and more fixated on the feeling of his muscular chest pressed against my back, but he continued talking anyway. "The left side is called port and the right side starboard."

Noted and categorized.

"The thing you're holding is a steering wheel. Kind of like a car, but not really. The wheel in your car controls the tires, a boat doesn't have tires."

I tilted my face toward him and rolled my eyes at his mention of the obvious.

"Fine, Miss Smarty Pants. Why don't you tell me what the wheel controls?" He smirked in a way that made me want to feel his breath on my cheek again.

"Just because I don't like boats doesn't mean I don't know the basics of how they work." Wishing I could forget about the boat and just bask in Greg's warmth, I released my grip on the wheel and traced the top of his hand with my fingertips. Only about a half a second slipped by before I reconnected with reality and my anxieties took back over. Gripping the wheel intently, I anchored my focus on the bow and focused on the water in front of us.

He pressed his lips to my temple and slid his hands on top of mine. "Relax. You're doing just fine."

I pushed the air out of my chest, drawing in a deep, audible breath then releasing it again. I was fine. I could do this. I took in another lung-penetrating breath then willed myself to relax my death grip on the wheel. It was just water and hundreds—probably thousands—of pounds of steel and fiberglass. Not to mention the weight of the people. And the added weight of the fish. Mine alone had nearly outweighed me . . . My thoughts raced in harmony with my increasing heartbeat.

As if he sensed my reemerging tension, Greg whispered his encouragement. "You can do this."

He was right. I could do anything. Anything, that is, but ever be comfortable and at ease on a boat.

Greg helped me guide the boat back toward the dock, patiently allowing me to steer the ship. From time to time he'd present me with the functions of each switch and lever on the dash. When he'd worked his way through all of those, he moved on to the rules of the water, or as he called them, the maritime guidelines and laws.

The hull of the boat cut its way upstream, against the current with almost no effort. The return trip seemed faster than the outbound one. Perhaps it was that the sun was out, or maybe because I wasn't freezing on the bow, but I think it was because of Greg's nearness. By the time we docked, my hands had quit trembling and my chest had quit thumping out of control.

Greg settled his arm over my shoulders and pulled

me in for a hug. "You did it," he whispered into my hair.

I smiled up at him, unsure that I could ever grow tired of looking at his gorgeous, rugged face. The wind carried the smell of fresh pine into the boat's cabin. Intermingled with Greg's cologne, it almost drowned out the ever-present stench of fish. His blond hair danced lightly in the cross-breeze, picking up the sun's rays as they pierced through the front window and bouncing them around playfully.

"Back to this business of you saying that you like me"—I stared into his deep blue eyes.

His lips curled up into a grin as he nodded the affirmative. "It's true."

"Good." I touched the soft bristles along his jawline. "Because I'm strongly leaning in the direction of liking you, too."

He raised his brow to a point. "Strong enough to leave behind everything you've ever known?"

I considered the question. What was I willing to sacrifice to quench my hunger? Could I leave behind my life in the city for one in the middle of nowhere? "Is that what it would take?"

His shoulders lifted lightly then fell again as he released a sigh. "Possibly. That's why I told you to dig deep for every ounce of information you could find on me. I would never feel right leading you into something blindly. You're here, which means you did some deep digging, but I'm pretty sure you didn't get deep enough." He slid his palm from my shoulder and down to my hand. "Don't get me wrong, Sam," he said as his fingers wrapped around mine. "I love you and would do anything to be able to be with you. But there are things you've yet to learn about me. Things you need to know before you make any kind of commitment."

"Yeah, about that." I was ready for the conversation. Ready to unload my questions and put my heart at ease. Ready for something other than the game of procrastinating that we'd played all day.

"I know." He nodded toward the fishing crew as they busily worked to unload the boat of themselves, their gear, and their catch. "Is there a way I can satiate your questions for just a bit longer? I'd prefer to answer them in private."

"You could kiss me," I blurted out, surprising even myself with my brashness.

His eyes locked with mine, sending ripples through my chest as he shortened the distance between us. "I was beginning to think you'd never ask."

"And I was beginning to think you'd never offer."

He slid his hand back up to my shoulder then onto the base of my neck, wrapping his fingers warmly over the back of my head. "I will happily concede to your wish only if you promise not to let it cloud your judgement. I need for you to be able to make a sound decision based on the facts."

"Don't I always?" No. The answer was no. At least not with him. In every other aspect of my life, it was a resounding yes. But with Greg . . .

I could feel the rhythm of my heart in my throat as he touched his lips to mine. Soft. Tender. Safe.

It was easy to shut out all my questions while I was enveloped in the warmth of his affection. I wrapped my hands around his collar, holding on to the moment with such ferocity I almost forgot that I even had questions. Suddenly, the things I didn't know seemed less important than the way he made me feel.

I held my eyes closed, cherishing the moment, as he slowly pulled his lips away from mine. "How was that?" he asked.

Fantastic. Exhilarating. Everything I thought it would be and more!

"I guess it will work for a little bit." I shrugged, playfully pretending that my whole body wasn't buzzing. "Eventually, however, I'm going to need more."

"More kisses?" He cupped my face in his palms.

My heart raced. "Yes. And more answers."

"Good. On both counts." He reached down and took hold of my hand, interlocking his fingers around mine. "I just hope my answers don't scare you."

"I don't see how they could."

"The fact that you're here, thousands of miles from home, on a boat, tells me that you're a pretty brave girl. It takes a lot of courage to push past your fears and take them head on."

"Is that what you think I'm doing with you? Taking on my fears?"

"If you know everything there is to know, then yes.

If you're not at least a little intimidated by my past, then you've got your blinders on." He gave my hand a gentle squeeze. "But, at the same time, maybe I'm wrong. Maybe you're tougher than me. I mean, I know what it took for you to get on this boat. You had legitimate fears and you conquered them. I have the utmost respect for that."

"Is it that obvious that I don't like boats?" I asked facetiously.

"No," he grinned that radiant smile that made me want to feel his lips on mine again. "Not at all. It's completely normal to death-grip the railing and lose all the color in your face when riding on a boat. And everybody sits as far away from the edge and hugs their knees to their chest. Totally normal."

I didn't know if there could possibly be anything worse than a day on a boat. But I'd survived over six hours on the open water. I hadn't puked or passed out or even cried. Anything Greg had left to share certainly had to be less scary than that.

"Should I be afraid of your secrets?" I asked as he started to walk away.

"Only you can decide that." He looked at the ground and shrugged. "First, I need to know what you found, then we can go from there. But not here—not now. I need to help these guys get stuff cleaned up. I know it's a lot to ask, and I've already asked so much of you today, but can you hold on just a little bit longer?"

"Just ensure me that my trust hasn't been

misplaced." I swallowed back the insecurities that had begun to race through my mind. There were holes in his personal data that definitely triggered uncertainty. I still didn't know why his records were hidden or why—or better yet, who—had gone through such trouble to wipe them, but those facts were pale in consideration of the warning he seemed to be issuing or the less-than-warm welcome I'd received for the better part of the day. Why, after all we'd shared in Utah, had he been so hesitant to let me in today? He'd kept me at arm's length for hours. Was he just playing nice now, kissing me and making my knees buckle as if it was a game? Was he hoping to send me running back home? I wanted to trust him, wanted to feel a connection, but his standoffish behavior was making it difficult.

He tucked his hands in his pockets and looked into my eyes as if reading all my insecurities. "It's not. I would never hurt you. I hope you believe that."

"I want to." With every breath I took, I wanted to. I wasn't afraid of him, but I certainly wanted to trust him. I wanted to know the man—the *real* man—behind the beautiful eyes and mesmerizing smile. I wanted to feel his warm embrace and experience the thrill of his kisses without having to wonder what he was hiding or if it was real.

But what if I didn't like what he had to tell me? What if his concerns were legit? What if his secrets were too big for me to carry?

"Then give me a chance to prove it." His mouth

turned up in a crooked half-grin.

"Hey, Romeo," Austin's voice rang from the dock. "Can I get some help bringing this bad boy to shore?"

Greg offered me a nod, curt and polite, then turned to help Austin drag my giant fish to shore.

*   *   *

With the exception of me, each member of the excursion helped carry their own catch to shore, where it would first be secured under a large wooden Gone Fishin' Tours sign for photos, then cleaned, packaged, and prepped for shipping. Even if I'd wanted to, I'm quite certain I couldn't have carried my fish. An attempt would have left either me or the fish dragging through the dirt. Undoubtedly me.

Even without carrying anything other than myself, I couldn't manage to make the transition from the dock to the shore with grace or ease. As soon as my feet transitioned from the wood dock to solid ground, I stumbled.

My hands hit the dirt, catching my body before it did a complete plant into the soil. My pride didn't catch the same break. Greg, Austin, and the fishing buddies hadn't seen me, but both the ladies watching from the deck of the fishing cabin had.

As if we shared some secret bond, the girl who'd met me in the tavern the night before slowly walked toward me. "Sometimes it can take a while to get your sea legs." Jacey said loud enough for the other woman to hear but soft enough that the men could not. "Are you okay?"

Dusting the dirt off my palms, I drew in a deep sigh. "Yes. Just my fine old clumsy self. Thanks for not making a scene."

She stepped close enough to drop her voice to a whisper. "I see that you chose not to follow my advice and invited yourself along this morning."

"Actually," I defended, "Greg invited me." Kind of. But really, what was her deal? Why was she so oppositional to me wanting to be around her brother?

"I was only trying to protect you. When you figure out what you're getting into, I expect you'll understand." She put her hand on my shoulder and directed me toward the other woman. "Mom," she started with a grin, "this is Greg's friend Samantha."

The tall woman rested one hand on her ample hip and another on the cabin's rustic log railing. Long wavy hair fell over her shoulders and about half way down her back. She had a splattering of gray, but for the most part her dark hair and pale skin made her look young. She shifted her hand on the railing and looked me over.

"Samantha," Jacey continued with a smile, "this is KJ Knight, my mom."

The older lady nursed a stiff leg down the cabin

steps and took a slightly hobbled step toward me. "It's nice to meet you."

"And you, too." I extended my hand toward her.

Ignoring my invitation for a handshake, she took another staggered step toward me and threw her arms warmly around me. "You can call me Kristen," she said. "I hope your visit has been nice so far."

"It has," I answered, and not just because I was enamored by her son. "It's absolutely beautiful here." The thick forests, clean air, and crystal clear skies were awe inspiring. Nature had made her masterpiece in Alaska, for sure.

"We love it." Kristen stepped back and looked me squarely in the eyes. "I hope you feel welcome for as long as you're here."

"Thank you." I found myself wondering if my two-and-a-half-day trip would lead to something more. I'd come with the intention of hooking my man, but hadn't really thought through what that would mean. For us to work, would I have to settle here? He'd just asked me if I was willing to leave behind everything I'd ever known—is that what he expected?

"I understand that trophy catch is yours." Kristen nodded toward the giant fish Greg and Austin had hung beneath the big Gone Fishin' sign.

"Yes." I nodded, feeling a strange sense of pride about the fish I really hadn't cared to catch.

"Well then, let's go get your photo with him so we can package up the meat and send it back home for you."

In my mind I made a joke about how Greg was the only trophy I was interested in taking home, but I didn't share it. Instead, I followed Kristen and Jacey's lead toward the large wooden sign where all of our catch from the day had been hung.

"You're just in time, pumpkin." Don took my hand and pulled me into their group shot alongside the fresh fish gallery. I held my breath against the smell of seaweed, fish, and sweaty old men while I forced a smile. Austin snapped a series of pictures with his phone.

I eyed my fish with a combination of awe and disgust. It hung by its gills, large and proud against the other halibut that hung beside it. From tip to tail it stood taller than me and, based on the fact that its tailfin grazed the ground, taller than most normal catches Greg and his crew drug in.

"I guess I ought to document this moment. I'm sure my dad would be so very pleased." Any father would claim bragging rights over such a catch. Mine especially. I was sure he'd have it framed and hung at the front of his store for all to see. Plus, it'd give me license to remind him that I wasn't a hermit. I did leave my house. And I was clearly not desperate or lonely.

"Here," I said, pulling my cell out of my pocket. "Will you take one of me with that beast?"

"Hold on," Greg said, signaling for me to hold on to my phone for a minute. He lifted his own phone up and instructed me to smile. I obeyed, then tried again to hand him my phone just as a text buzzed through.

I looked down at the buzzing apparatus in my hand, then questioningly at Greg. "How did you know my number?" I asked, confused by the photo of me and my fish that had shown up on my screen.

"I know pretty much everything there is to know about you." He said the words—and by all accounts, they should've seemed creepy—but he didn't give me time to question before he had me hypnotized in his warm gaze.

Either I was stupidly in love or stupidly naïve. "About that," I said as I willingly melted into his trance. "I mean, about what we know—and don't know—about each other."

He took my hand and turned toward Kristen, Jacey, and Austin. "I know it's Jack's day off, but I called him and asked if he could help prep the fish. He should be here soon. Can you handle things without me for a bit?"

"You didn't ask him to run your evening salmon run, too, did you?" Jacey asked with a frown.

"No. Just to help clean. Couple hours tops, then he can go back to enjoying his day off."

My heart jumped. I was getting my time.

Mine. Alone. Finally.

CHAPTER NINE

Greg led me behind the fishing cabin and onto a trail that shadowed the river bank. His fingers entwined around mine as if they were meant to fit together. My heart raced as every question that had formed over the last several weeks began to fight for first position in my mind.

But what if he couldn't answer my concerns? And, more so, what if I didn't like his answers? Was the rational part of my mind strong enough to overpower the rush of excitement he caused to pulse through me? And what about the sense of peace and belonging he encouraged within me?

There was only one way to know.

"Why does your mom have a limp?" Of all the

questions that'd spent weeks burning up my thoughts, how had one of such little importance surfaced to the top?

"That's your big burning question?" The irony of it apparently wasn't mine alone. He raised his brow. "She was involved in a fishing accident. Big old halibut threw himself across the deck and broke her hip."

"Ouch! Are you serious?"

He nodded.

I flinched at the image in my mind. No wonder he hadn't attempted to wrestle with my fish. He hadn't been kidding about the halibut's strength. The gun suddenly made a new level of sense.

He stared at me, a sideways grin creeping over his face. "Somehow I don't think you came all this way to ask fish questions."

I twisted my lips. "Yeah. Maybe that wasn't the right place to start." Like ants scurrying to get out of a hole, my thoughts scrambled to push themselves to the surface. I bit my lip and drew a deep breath.

"Why can't you go to that bar? Why are your records buried? And why are half of them missing?" I stopped walking and turned to look at him. "Why so many secrets?"

"Now we're getting somewhere." He cupped his free hand over our intertwined ones. "I'm sorry you had to work so hard, but I really am glad you found me."

"Me, too . . . I think."

"I hope so." He directed me to a large rock just off

the side of the walking path and indicated for me to sit down. After I was situated on the hard, cold surface, he settled in beside me. "I promise to answer your questions, Sam. I can't promise you'll like the answers, but I won't lie to you." His eyes, as if offering an invitation to believe him, pierced mine.

"Okay." I swallowed the lump in my throat. Even he was worried about what I'd think of his truths. "I'm not sure exactly where to start."

"Why don't you tell me what you know first and we'll go from there?"

That sounded reasonable. I folded my arms across my chest and tucked my hands tightly into the crease of my elbows. Though reasonably warm in the sunshine, a tall pine cast its heavy shadow over our rock, dropping the temperature enough to make my fingers cold. "I know you have at least five aliases: Seth, Jeffrey, Kevin, Allen, and, well, Gregory. But I think Gregory is your real name. Maybe. Either that or you've done a good job building a fake family and a fake life for him."

Greg settled his hand on my knee, his eyes continued to lock mine. "Gregory is the name I was given at birth." He smirked. "And as much as I'd like to not claim Jacey some days, she is my real sister and Kristen is my real mom. So, yes, you've gotten that part right."

"And your dad? I don't"—

He broke eye contact for brief moment then, directing his gaze back toward me, answered somberly,

"What I told you on the boat was true. He's gone. Lost him to cancer when I was sixteen. That's when my mom, Jacey, and I took over the fishin' business."

"I'm sorry."

"No worries."

"So, who ran the company when you were off in Utah?"

"Mom and Jacey." He shrugged as if it were no big deal for a team of women to run fishing excursions. "And Jack. Mostly Jack. He's Mom's friend."

I processed the new information.

"Come on Sam, that's the easy stuff. What else do you know?"

"I know you enlisted with the Navy when you were eighteen."

"Yes."

"And you trained as a Navy SEAL."

"Also correct."

It almost felt like a game—me asserting facts, him validating them. Almost too easy. Too smooth. I chewed at my lip as I made verbal classification to my next observation. "You served several years and seemed to get a lot of recognition but then, completely out of the blue, your military records disappeared."

"So you couldn't find them?"

"No, I found them, but they weren't complete. After a certain date, they've been blacked out."

"I see. And what do you make of that?"

That was the hard part—I wasn't comfortable

drawing conclusions about things I knew virtually nothing about. I hated that the data was thin. I wanted concrete facts and indisputable evidence. I had neither. "I think it's in relation to you being court-martialed." I finally offered the tidbit of information Jacey had shared with me. "But I didn't find any data about a court-martial, so I don't know if or when it fits in to the whole picture." I twisted my lips nervously and looked at him for clarification.

"If you're asking if there was a court-martial, the answer is yes."

"What was it for?"

He directed his eyes to the ground, kicking at a pile of fallen pine needles, but didn't answer.

"Why were you court martialed?" I asked again. "And is it connected to your vanishing identity?"

He kicked the pine needles one more time then tilted his head enough for me to see the hesitation in his eyes.

I wasn't sure if he was stalling or if I'd dug into some details that made him uncomfortable. It didn't matter. I wanted answers. Needed them.

"And what about Bart's Tavern? How's that connected? And Utah? Why were you there? Who really hired you? Because, if it had been Rushton, you should have been indicted with him, right? But if it wasn't him, then who? Ugh!" I threw my hands in the air. The more I thought I knew the less sense it all made.

"It sounds like you've definitely done your

homework. I expected nothing less. Well done." He squeezed my knee as if assuring me of his approval. "Before I bombard you with my answers, do you mind if I ask you one question?"

My heart raced with anticipation. I was excruciatingly ready to solve the Seth puzzle. I didn't want to stall any longer. "Fine," I conceded. "Just one."

"How exactly did you find me?"

"From your military records."

"But you said they were missing."

"Well, they were. Then we found them. Buried deep behind security clearances and dark servers."

"We?"

"Yes. Me and my coworker, David."

"And from them you were able to find where I live?"

"Kind of. Your enlistment papers were attached, but those records weren't conclusive. I had to pull other data to verify the finite details."

"How did you get the clearance to see what you saw?"

"First, this is definitely more than one question. And second, I may or may not have bypassed typical security protocol."

"Thank you for humoring me." He patted my knee. "Last question: could you have found the information you needed without being an insider?"

I reworked the situation in my mind. "I don't know." I shook my head. "Maybe. It would have been hard, but not impossible. First of all, data never really disappears. If someone was desperate enough—and smart enough—they could eventually piece together enough crumbs to form the same conclusions that I did. Having government clearance was key, but if I hadn't had it, I could've social engineered it. Would've taken a lot longer and I would've really had to push out of my comfort zone, but people do it every day."

"You're brilliant."

"No, not really. There are still whole chunks of your information missing. We're not talking about a low-level erase job or a computer glitch, either. Someone who knew what they were doing went through a lot of effort to intentionally black it out. But who? And why?"

"I said you were brilliant, not a magician. I'd like to try to help you fill in the blanks, but you have to promise not to jump too quickly to conclusions about who—or what—I am. Okay?"

I nodded, eager to finally be getting somewhere.

"Okay." Adjusting himself on the rock, he looked over both shoulders, then down the trail from the direction we came. When he finally spoke, it was in a tone so hushed I had to lean in to hear him. "Some of the information I'm about to tell you is top secret and I don't mean that in a teasing or casual way. Top secret, as in government classified. If you leak it, the consequences could be fatal. To me. To my family. And especially to you." He squeezed my hands. "I don't know about you, but I definitely don't want that to happen."

I nodded. I got it. But maybe I didn't want to get it. Maybe I should've gotten up and walked away. The less I knew, the less liability I had toward both my safety and Greg's, too.

"So, as you know I was a Navy SEAL. I served many tours and killed many people."

He paused long enough for the gravity of his words to settle. They were heavy. I made a mental note that he'd used the word 'many,' though I wasn't sure assigning a quantifying value changed anything.

"I don't love taking people out or spilling blood," he continued. "But I do not apologize for helping make the world a safer place." He paused and looked me directly in the eyes. "Samantha, I need you to honestly ask yourself if you're okay with that."

When I opened my mouth to respond he placed a finger over my lips and shook his head. "I don't want an off-the-cuff answer. And I don't want you to tell me what you think I want to hear. I need you to be honest because, frankly, my military actions may be the least troubling thing I tell you today."

The pounding in my chest came to a dead halt and my shoulders tensed as I considered his request. An eagle soared effortlessly above us, cutting a peaceful path across the blue sky. I watched it in flight, yearning for the same calm he seemed to have. "I knew you were a SEAL before I ever booked my flight," I said after a few minutes of silence. "I don't love guns or violence, but I can't say that war-time actions are in the same category as murder. As you know, my dad was in the military, too. I never asked him if he'd killed anyone and he never told me. I suppose the same applies to you. I will never ask and I don't expect you to tell me."

"So, regardless of what they may or may not be, you're okay with my war-time engagements?"

"I have an understanding of what it takes to secure our freedom."

"What about non-war-time casualties?"

On a certain level I knew, or at least suspected, that he might be a gun-for-hire. He'd admitted to being hired to kill me during my rendezvous in Utah. I'd tried not to overthink the details of that admission, but it was something I needed clarification on and time to process. "Are you talking about your job as a hit-man?"

"I am a trained killer and I've earned a reputation for being very good at what I do, but I have my limits. Technically speaking, I am not a hit-man. Sometimes I pretend to be, but at the core, I am not."

"I'm not sure what you mean."

"I've never killed someone for money. But"—his eyes darted away from mine and he looked down at the ground. "Remember how you asked why I couldn't go to the bar?"

"Yes."

"It's not that I can't. At least in terms of the fact that I'm not forbidden. I could walk through those doors and nobody in this town would try to stop me or think less of me for it. No one, except me, that is." He shook his head.

I wasn't sure where he was headed but the heaviness of his brows and the sinking of his face suggested that it was painful. He anchored his gaze to the ground and paced from one side to the other.

"A few years ago my life took a huge turn—and I can't say it was for the better. I'd just gotten back from Afghanistan. It'd been a highly intense tour and to be honest, I wasn't in a good psychological place. Things had been ugly in the desert and all I wanted was to come home, kick back on my boat, and decompress." He slid his hands into his jeans' pockets and looked out across the river.

"Jacey was pregnant. Just a couple of months along. Her boyfriend was a guy she'd known from school. He'd always seemed like a pretty decent guy." He shrugged his shoulders and let out a loud sigh. "They got into a disagreement the night I got home. Something about money and the baby and whatever. He lost control and took it out on my sister."

He pulled his hands out of his pockets and balled them in to fists. "I'd just settled in to bed when the doorbell rang. Exhausted from my travel, I rolled to my side and pulled a pillow over my head. It wasn't until my mom opened the door that I heard Jacey's frantic cries for help. He'd beaten her up—broken her jaw, bruised her up good, then dumped her on my mom's porch and ran like the coward he was."

Rage ran through me. "What kind of man would do

that to a woman? A pregnant woman, none-the-less?"

Greg grunted out a sigh. "After we rushed Jacey to the hospital, I went to find the guy. It didn't take long. He'd hunkered down at Bart's Tavern, tossing back one drink after another while my sister was in surgery. I walked into that bar with a chip on my shoulder and score to settle. It wasn't okay to hurt my sister—or any girl. Not like that. Not like he did."

"Did you hit him?" I asked, thinking that's what I'd have done.

"I killed him."

The tightening of my jaw appeared almost as poignant as the sudden pain in my gut. My hands were instantly sweaty and shaking in my jacket pockets. I buckled over and choked on the lump in my throat. "You what?"

Greg stared at the ground for several, silent moments. "I told you the truth wasn't pretty," he sighed. "As soon as he saw me, he barreled his chest and started in. In between his fits of laughter, he said some really awful things about my sister. He called her names I'd been taught to never use and made light of her—their—pregnancy. Said he never wanted a kid, and a lot of that sort of garbage. Then he took another shot of his drink and thought it would be a good idea to take a swing at me. Before I knew it he was trying to push me up into the wall, so I punched him. A few times. Hard."

"But that doesn't…"

"It only took three punches before his body went limp and his knees collapsed. When he hit the floor I walked away. I had no interest in watching him grovel." The color had all but drained out of Greg's face. There was moisture in his eyes as he looked at me. "I didn't know that he was dead until the sheriff showed up in Jacey's hospital room to take me away."

My mind spun in circles, trying to weave its way through the details. I replayed his story through my mind, nauseated by the details. "I don't get it," I finally said. "All you did was punch him?"

"You don't go through the kind of training I've been through and throw a punch like a high school bully. I'm a SEAL, Sam, and I used exactly the kind of combat tactics that a special ops agent is trained to use. Only, I wasn't in a war situation nor was I justified to use that kind of force. The sheriff turned me over to my CO and a general court-martial was empowered against me. I was charged with manslaughter."

Manslaughter. Bile filled my throat. It was an ugly word with even uglier implications. It wasn't murder, but he had taken a life. With his own hands. Unsolicited by war.

Maybe I didn't really want to know his secrets after all.

CHAPTER TEN

I made fists of my trembling hands and shoved them as deep into my jacket pockets as they would go. "Well," I whispered the words with pretend confidence, "they must've found you not-guilty or you wouldn't be here, right?" I feigned a smile but on the inside I was churning.

He pitched his shoulders backwards and stood up straight. "No, I was guilty. Every day of my life I will be guilty. My training kicked in and I lost control. I killed a man with my bare hands. And not just any man, my sister's boyfriend. My nephew's father."

"But it wasn't intentional." I defended him, though my emotions were roller coasting out of control.

STEPHANIE CONNELLEY WORLTON

"You're right, it wasn't, but that doesn't change the fact that I did it. I'm a dangerous man, Sam. I think it's only fair that you know that."

"If you were dangerous, why would they let you walk free?" I was grasping at straws, as if justifying his actions would somehow change the ugly reality of what he'd done.

"I wouldn't exactly say I'm free. You were right about someone with power and influence messing around with my records. For whatever reason, that same someone considered me an asset. He took confidence in my skill set and thought our country would be better served under a new contract rather than locking me away in a cell. I am free because of that contract—and I'm grateful for it—but the terms aren't always convenient or pretty."

"So, the records?" I wondered out loud. "Are they trying to protect you or is it more about hiding what you did?"

"Both." He rubbed his hand across his chin stubble. "As far as the government is concerned, the court-martial never existed. Coincidently, neither does Gregory Knight anymore."

"And what about the aliases?" I was trying desperately to make sense of it all.

"Part of my contract."

"And your time in Utah?" I held my breath.

"Also part of the contract."

The more I learned, the less it all made sense. He

102

was a SEAL, then he wasn't. He should be locked up, but he wasn't. He worked for the government but Peter Rushton had hired him to kill me. "I don't understand how this all connects. What does any of this have to do with Peter Rushton? I thought you worked for him."

"I did."

"But you said you work for the government."

"Yes."

"Which is it?"

"Both."

Both? I was trying to understand but things just weren't clicking. Maybe my mind was too tired to process it all, or maybe it was just too much for a simple, computer geek, hermit to fathom.

"Both?" So, what does that make you? A double-agent or something?" I suddenly wished I'd have read more spy novels as kid.

"I'm going to go with the 'or something' on this one."

I buried my face in my hands and closed my eyes, trying to wrap my mind around everything he'd told me. Navy SEAL. Manslaughter. Court-martial. Each detail impressed itself in my brain, waiting for categorization. Government contracts and cover-ups and 'or somethings'—I didn't even know how to process those. He'd promised me truths, but it still felt like secrets to me. Too many secrets.

I uncovered my face and studied the man in front of me. My heart still wanted to cling on to him, my brain, however, wasn't so sure.

He glanced at his watch then took my hands in his. "I'm sorry, Sam. I know this is a lot to take in." He gripped my hands firmly, yet with a gentleness that made it hard to believe they were the same hands that had killed a man. "I'm sure you still have questions, and I want you to have your answers. But I've just unloaded a lot of heavy information on you. I think it'd be good for you to process what I've told you so far—as in, really think it through and decide how you feel about it. Am I right?"

"Probably." Definitely. I needed to take a breath—or five-hundred—and sort through everything. And I needed to do it without the mesmerizing power of his presence. As long as I could see him—feel his warmth, smell his musk, and be hypnotized by his movements—I wouldn't be able to separate rational logic from unquantifiable emotion.

"I think you know how I feel about you, Sam, and I suspect you have had some of the same feelings about me. But please consider what I've told you. I can't let you dive into things blindly. You deserve to know what you're getting into."

I nodded in agreement. We were clearly on the same page with that. I was a plotter and a planner. Rational, thoughtful, and calculating.

"A relationship with me," he continued, "is not just inconvenient but dangerous. If you're looking for a fairytale happily-ever-after, I can't offer that. At least not until my contract is fulfilled. And, even then, I'm afraid that I will always be a soldier."

He wasn't doing a very good job trying to secure my devotion. "Are you trying to tell me that you don't want me to love you?" My lip quivered.

"I don't think it's possible to tell a heart who to love and who not to love. But if that's where you're leaning. . ." He sighed deeply. "I don't want you to go in blind. Loving me comes with concessions. When I get a call I have to drop everything and leave. I could disappear in the middle of the night and be gone for weeks— months even—without being able to call you. I live a top secret life and, let's be honest, it's not a fair situation to put a girlfriend or a wife through."

"I see," I answered, though I didn't really see anything. I'd emptied my savings account, put my job and sanity and maybe even safety on the line to chase him. And he wasn't sure it was a good thing for me to be involved in his life?

I bit my lip and swallowed the giant lump of frustration in my chest. "If you didn't want to open the door," I asked through muffled tears, "then why did you encourage me to find you?"

"That's a valid question."

I was trying to be mad at him, but the soft way his eyes pierced mine made it difficult.

"Truth is," he said in a muted tone, "I let my feelings override my judgement. I didn't mean to, but I fell in love with you. There isn't anything that brings me more joy than idea of being with you. But," he sighed the word, "I've come to realize how selfish that is."

My eyes started to warm. "So would you prefer me to leave?" The words trembled over my lips.

"Oh, Sam." He cupped my face in his palms. "No, I don't want you to leave, but I can't ask you to stay either. This little slice of Alaska is my heaven, but it's only a small fragment of my life. If this were everything I had to offer, I'd be on my knees begging you to up your life and join me. But it's not. The life I live is not a safe one. I'm always on guard, especially when it comes to the people I love. My mom, and Jacey, and Clay." His jaw squared and his eyes glazed over for a second time. "You have no idea what it's like to know you're the reason a kid doesn't have a father." He shook his head and drew a deep breath. "That kid is my sunshine and I'd do anything for him. But he's also a liability. There are people after me who wouldn't bat an eye at hurting my family. Jacey and my mom have had to learn to cope with it. They're always on alert, constantly looking over their shoulders, because they have to be. They've been through special training. They carry weapons. That's what it's like being a part of my life. They didn't have a choice in the matter, but you do."

"And if I choose you?"

He shook his head. "I can't let you make that kind of decision on the fly. You need to put some serious thought into it. You need to ask yourself if this is what you really want. And you need to be honest about it."

A tear burned its way over my cheek and down to the corner of my mouth. He watched it flow but neither of us attempted to wipe it away. I opened my mouth to respond, but couldn't find any words to express what I was feeling. What was I feeling? Hurt? Angry? Rejection? I didn't know.

He glanced at his watch again, drawn between me and the responsibilities of running a company. "I've got a salmon trip to captain in about ten minutes," he sighed. "As much as I'd love to take you with me, I think you need some time to think. And maybe a little time for a nap, too."

He was right—on both accounts. I was running on fumes and maybe a touch of desperation. The last twenty-four hours—thirty-six, really—had been almost overwhelming. Airplanes and boats and giant fish were just the tip of my iceberg. Finding Greg, not finding Greg, kissing Greg, learning he'd committed manslaughter. I was exhausted just thinking about it all. One more stress in my day would probably break me. "Do I really look that bad?" I rubbed at my eyes.

"You look beautiful."

I cocked my head and raised a brow. "No more lies, remember."

"It's not a lie. You are stunning. But you're also tired. I can see it in your eyes. You've had a long day and I just dropped a whole lot on your plate that you need to process." He pulled his Jeep keys out of his pocket and settled them in my hand. "Why don't you go back to the hotel and take a nap while I do my salmon run? I'll be back to shore around nine o'clock. If you're still interested in pursuing this little thing we've started, come get me."

"And if I don't show?" The words trembled past my lips. Had I come this far to leave empty handed? My heart couldn't handle the possibility.

"Then tuck the keys under the driver's seat and I'll have Jacey pick it up later." He reached for my hand. "Do you want to walk back with me?"

"Actually," I said, "I think I'd like to sit here for a minute and gather my thoughts."

"Understood." He leaned down and kissed my forehead before walking away.

I sat, almost as still as the rock I was perched on, and watched the man who'd filled my dreams walk away.

CHAPTER ELEVEN

From my stoop I caught sight of Greg's tin boat as it drifted down the river. In my numbness, I watched it steadily float by, then disappear around the river's bend. He had four, maybe five passengers, but I hadn't really counted. My entire focus had been on him. How could a man so seemingly kind and gentle, have the monstrous life he claimed to have?

Stretching my legs down to the ground, I settled my feet onto the same bed of pine needles that I'd watched Greg kick around. I measured each breath in increments of perceived pain. Not being able to quantify what was happening to me, I took a deep breath of the pine-scented air, and pushed my hands into the pocket of my hoodie.

My mind and my heart had never opposed each other with such ferocity. I clasped Greg's Jeep keys in my hand and willed my feet to move back down the path. The silence in the adjacent forest made me uneasy. I hugged the side of the path closest to the river, taking comfort in the rushing sound of its flowing waters. Though I had no reason to be afraid of Greg, he'd made sure I knew a life that involved him was one full of risk. Had I already put myself in danger's path simply by coming here?

A branch cracked behind me and I jerked my head quickly around to look for it. I saw nothing. Not a bird in the trees nor a squirrel on the ground. Taking in another deep draw of the crisp air, I steadied my gate forward.

By the time I pulled the Jeep into the hotel parking lot, I'd lost complete perspective on reality. I pushed the door to my room open and fell onto the bed. I closed my eyes, but the tornado in my mind was too strong to cave to my exhaustion. I stared at the ceiling, attempting to silence my thoughts so I could rest, but it was fruitless. My questions weren't going to go anywhere until I plotted them out.

Wishing I'd brought a laptop, I settled for the small notepad and pen on the hotel's bedside table. One at a time I jotted down the data Greg had given me.

Navy SEAL. I immediately put a check beside the bullet point. I'd done my research on this point before leaving home, there was no need to reanalyze it. People who loved their country joined the military. Check.

Manslaughter. It almost hurt to write the word. I offered a sigh to the walls, then worked my way through the details. Greg had strong, powerful, fierce hands and intensive training to use them as weapons. He'd used them in a fit of anger. On a certain level I found reason to justify his actions, but that didn't erase the concern they raised. Was Greg harboring uncontrolled rage? Did he have unresolved PTSD? Would he ever unleash his anger on me? What about our kids?

Our kids? How had I jumped to that point? All I wanted was to be with the guy, see where the tingles and butterflies might lead, and all of a sudden I'd jumped to kids. I played with the thought for a few moments, twisting it through the scenarios my mind busily created. Greg had asked me to seriously consider the future. If kids weren't serious, I didn't know what was. As distant as the possibility felt, kids were a potential part of our future.

I didn't know for sure, had no concrete evidence to draw a conclusion either way, but my gut told me Greg wasn't dangerous. I doodled over the ugly word's bullet point, tracing over it again and again until it became a large, bold arrow.

Not bothering to slide shoes on my feet, I opened my hotel room door and stepped out into the short shadows of the late afternoon. Across the way, the parking lot for Bart's Tavern had started to fill. I looked away from it, not wanting to dwell on the images Greg's narrative had conjured. I didn't like thinking of him in that dark, smoky building, full of anger and . . . My stomach turned.

I wiped the image from my mind and focused my gaze on the concrete sidewalk between me and the hotel office. Stopping just below the flickering vacancy sign, I turned down the small hall that housed two vending machines and an old, noisy ice machine. Looking over the offerings, I settled on a chocolate cookie and can of ginger ale, then padded my way back to my room and my list.

I paused for a moment at the bold arrow I'd drawn then, without reading the word I knew was beside it, moved down to the next one.

Court-martial. Sigh. Uncool, but as far as the government was concerned, non-existent. I settled onto the bed. Greg could have left that detail out of his account and I'd have never known the difference. Nothing existed to prove his story one way or the other. But he'd chosen to tell me. That was something. I drew a check mark beside the bullet.

The next word was "contract." I drew a dash and wrote the word "classified" beside it. The question wasn't whether a contract existed, but whether or not I could live with the terms of it. Was it CIA? FBI? Some other less known entity?

I twirled the pen between my fingers, trying to decide if it mattered what agency actually employed him.

Clearly Greg was committed to fulfilling his obligations to whatever—or whomever—it was, even at the cost of his personal life, but could I do the same? Did I want to?

I skipped to the next bullet point. It contained three words: Love. Sacrifice. Danger. With Greg, apparently, they were synonymous. I fell back into the pillows and, closing my eyes, tuned in to the pounding in my chest. I counted my heart beat in measures of three. One, two, three. One, two, three. Love, sacrifice, danger.

*   *   *

I flinched awake, startled by the muffled sound of a vibration beside me. Still pitched against the stack of pillows along the headboard, I rolled the kink out of my neck as I ran my hand though the blankets in search of my phone.

"Hello," I said, still pulling out of my nap as I raised the phone to my ear.

"Hey, Samantha."

Todd. I glanced at the time on my phone's screen. Nearly 7:30 pm Alaska time. I did the math. That was 11:30 pm on the East Coast. "Hi, Todd."

"I know it's kind of late, I hope I didn't wake you."

"No," I lied. A girl my age, even one with as minimal of a social life as mine, had no excuse for being asleep before midnight on a Saturday night.

"Good." His voice was loud and energetic. "I was

hoping to catch you up."

"No worries. Of course I'm awake." Barely. I rolled my shoulders forward then arched my back and pulled myself to a full sitting position on the center of the bed. "What's up?"

"Well, I'm near Baltimore tonight doin' a gig and I had a little idea pop into my mind."

"Okay." I looked down at the bullet list lying beside me on the hard hotel mattress. I picked it up and smoothed it over my thigh.

"So, I'm about twenty minutes or so from your house. And, well, it'll be after 2:00 am by time we clean up and get out of here, but I thought maybe I could come crash at your house tonight."

Silence.

I ran my finger over the small note again, unsuccessfully trying to imagine Todd's flirtatious smile on the other end of the line. It was pointless. All I could see were Greg and a half-a-dozen red flags.

"No hanky-panky, I promise." Todd quickly interjected. "Just a blanket on the couch, that's all I'm asking for."

"Hmm." Our last encounter flooded my mind. The kiss we'd shared had been nice—not as passionate and fulfilling as a kiss with Greg—but nice. And safe.

"I'd like to take you out for breakfast in the morning," he rushed forward. "No strings attached. Just breakfast. Just friends." He paused just long enough for me to envision his facetious smile as he ran his hand over his forehead and through his long locks of hair. "Unless you'd like more."

I looked down at my little paper again. Love. Sacrifice. Danger . . . Manslaughter. Could Todd offer me something more comfortable? Something without concessions, or secrets, or the threat of danger?

"I'm not home." It was a good answer. A safe one. An honest one. One that left me wiggle room and the opportunity to keep Todd as a solid plan B. Suddenly I felt guilty. I was officially a player.

"Sweet. I hope you're out having a good time. What time will you be back? I don't mind waiting. I can even pick you up, if you'd like."

"No, I mean I'm not home. I'm out of town."

"Oh." Long pause. "I had no idea. Where'd you go?"

Ignoring the direct question, I answered circuitously. "I just needed to run away for a few days."

"Sure. That's great. Totally get it." He was nothing if not optimistic—and perhaps a little cocky. "Give me a call when you get back. I'd love to hear all about it."

After bidding our farewells, I opened my messages and saw the photo Greg had sent me. Either the fish looked ridiculously large or I looked ridiculously small and fragile. I chuckled at the image then sent it on to Todd. For good measure, I decided to forward it to David as well.

Scooting to the edge of the bed, I picked up my list and looked at it again. I couldn't drag Todd along for the ride, nor could I keep dragging myself along. It was decision time. Hard. Fast. Cut and dry, decision time.

I stared intently at the last word on my list before slapping the paper face down on the nightstand.

Secrets.

As part of my job with the NSA, I operated within the limits of secrets every day. How could I ask someone to share all their secrets with me if I couldn't share all of mine with them?

CHAPTER TWELVE

I emerged from the hotel room reenergized and rededicated to my purpose. A nap and a shower had been just the reboot I'd needed.

I looked at my bullet list one last time then tore it into shreds and deposited it in the trash bin just outside my door. If Jacey could forgive Greg for taking her son's father, then so should I. And, if his family could live within the bounds of his job responsibilities, then so could I. I had no false pretenses that it would be easy, but the thought of living without Greg forever was worse than the thought of sharing him with some government entity.

When I got in the Jeep I was immediately

comforted in my decision. A single, white lily—the same variety as the bouquet that had been sent to me at home—lay across the steering wheel. I didn't know how Greg got it there, since he was supposed to be occupied on a salmon fishing expedition, but it brought me joy nonetheless.

I picked up the flower, pressing it to my nose. The rich aroma was soft and soothing. I held it in my hands, observing its simplistic beauty, as I considered the path that had brought me to Alaska. Satisfied that Greg had sent the large bouquet to my home, I took comfort in the fact that he had kept tabs on me even when I hadn't yet figured out how to find him. He had no reason to do that unless his feelings were genuine. I took another deep breath of the floral perfume then gently rested the blossom onto the passenger seat.

When I pulled up in front of the fishing cabin, the slot where Greg docked the tin boat was still empty. The sun had disappeared over the horizon, but the sky still glowed with the final touches of its light. Figuring he'd be back soon, I parked his Jeep then climbed the wooden stairs to the cabin's entrance.

"Hello?" Jacey called as I pushed the creaking door open. She appeared in the office doorway, offering me a gracious smile.

"Hi," I called back, realizing how uncharacteristically comfortable I was in her presence despite the less than warm welcome she'd given me earlier. The butterflies that typically took over my stomach around new people were missing. So, too, was the trepidation I harbored against unsolicited conversation and the disinterest I generally had in being around other people.

She waved me back to the small room where she and her son were watching television. "Greg should be back soon," she said as if she'd never tried to hamper my efforts to see her brother. "The best fishing is usually right at twilight. As soon as the light starts to dissipate, he'll be headed back in." She turned her attention toward her son. The blue-eyed boy sat, cross-legged on the couch, snuggling a bowl of popcorn tightly in his arms. "Clay," she said, "this is Uncle Greg's friend, Samantha. Do you mind if she sits next to you?"

He looked my way suspiciously then, hugging his popcorn bowl protectively against his chest, climbed on his mom's lap. She laughed. "Sometimes he's a little shy." She pointed to the empty couch cushion. "Pull up a seat."

I settled into the vacant spot and, mindful not to scare the boy, took silent inventory of the photos that lined the walls. In the front of the store, there didn't seem to be any of Greg, but back in this private room, hung an assortment of pictures of a blonde-haired, blue-eyed cutie that were undeniably him. The collection spanned many years, from Greg's early childhood to his teen years. His enlistment photo hung prominently beside the TV.

We sat in comfortable silence—the kind that I truly

appreciated—Jacey and Clay watching a travel show about the world's most family friendly beaches, me absorbing every detail about Greg's early life that I could.

"I think I owe you an apology," Jacey finally cut into the silence. "I wasn't trying to be rude earlier—and I really don't have anything against you." She hugged her son tightly against her. "This life's not for everybody, you know. I guess I underestimated you. My brother cares for you very deeply and I'm assuming that you coming back tonight means the feelings must be mutual."

I nodded. There wasn't a secret on the planet that could make me want her brother any less. Every time he was near me, I felt complete in a way I never imagined possible. He filled a void I never knew existed before him.

"Because, without true, unselfish love," she continued, as if posing a warning, "no girl in her right mind would sign up for this."

I turned away from the photo of a teenaged, muscle-clad Greg holding up a string of salmon. "Thanks." I nodded, realizing the irony of falling for a guy who loved the very things I didn't. I didn't enjoy boats or deep water like he did, but there was a certain splendor and tranquility about the mountains, the lack of traffic, and the slower pace of life.

The door creaked open and Clay sprung from his mom's lap in a rush of excitement, flinging his popcorn across the couch. My own excitement mirrored his as soon as I heard Greg's voice. "Hey buddy." He scooped the exuberant toddler into his arms. "How was your day?"

The boy, who'd sat silent the whole time I'd been in the cabin, yammered on in quick, broken sentences about his trip to the park and his lunch with Grandma. He'd just started in on his new shoes when Greg's eyes caught mine.

He kissed the boy's cheek, whispered something in his ear, then set him back down on the ground. "Hi." He smiled as he moved toward me.

"Hi." My voice cracked and my heart raced. I stood from the couch, my knees wobbly, my chest pounding.

"You look stunning." He took both of my hands in his. "And rested."

"I took a nap." I smiled. "And a shower," I added, though the words felt silly coming out of my mouth.

Unfazed by my awkwardness, he gave my hands a gentle squeeze and stared deep into my eyes. "You came back."

"Of course."

"I'm assuming . . ."

I cut him off. "You don't need to assume anything." My lip trembled. "I've thought it through and . . ."

It was his turn to cut me off. "And you're here. That's all I need to know." He raised his hands to my face then traced his fingers down my cheek before settling them on my jaw. He lightly nudged my chin up, guiding my eyes to meet his as he drew his thumb tenderly across my trembling lips. His eyes said more than words ever could and, as he pressed his lips to mine, I knew I'd made the right choice.

"I'd like to show you something spectacular," he whispered, his lips brushing lightly against mine.

I traced the contours of his muscular chest with my fingers. I was already looking at something spectacular. "Okay." I smiled eagerly.

"There's a lunar eclipse tonight and I guarantee there will be a show like nothing you've ever seen before." He slid his hands over my shoulders then down to the small of my back, pulling my body even closer to his. His heart pounded against my chest, matching rhythm with mine.

"Okay," I answered again, convinced I'd go to the moon and back just to be in his presence.

"But"—he paused his thought long enough to plant another kiss on my lips— "it involves a little boat ride. In the dark. And the cold. Are you game?"

My stomach did a somersault as my mind worked through the equation. Boat plus water plus darkness. "On the big boat or the little boat?"

"Well, the big one is more comfortable, but"—he winked—"the little one is more romantic."

"Why do you have to put it like that? You know there is no way I'm getting on that little tin can."

"So you pick comfort over romance?" He drew his hands up the base of my neck until they disappeared into my hair.

The thrill of his touch swept over my body. "I pick comfort over a panic attack."

"If you trust me, then you have nothing to fear though, right?"

There it was, point blank. The big question. Did I trust him fully, without reservation?

I wrapped my arms securely around him and looked up in to his eyes. "Okay," I said, biting my lower lip. "The little, tin-trap of a boat it is."

"Great." He leaned over and kissed me again. His fingers tickled over the lobe of my ear and down to the nape of my neck. "Why don't you stay put for a minute in here while I get things ready."

"Okay," I said with a sigh. It was now or never. I had to prove—not just to Greg, but to myself—that I was willing to trust him.

"I'll be back in about five." He pulled my hands off his chest, kissed the top of them, then turned toward the door. "Maybe Jacey can get you a heavier jacket," he called over his shoulder as the door swung closed behind him.

I paced the floor, trying to settle my nerves. "It will be okay," I whispered to myself. It was only a boat. Only water. And Greg was a SEAL. If a SEAL couldn't keep me safe on the water, then who could?

"What's going on?" Jacey nodded at the television as she settled a coat over my shoulders.

I'd been so busy repeating self-assertions that I'd

forgotten that the TV was even on. "I'm not sure." Sliding my arms into the coat, I turned toward the screen.

A ticker flashed at the bottom of the display. "Breaking news from Soldotna," it said.

A casually dressed news anchor repeated the same tagline as the camera swung to show his position on the shoulder of a forested road. "Officials located what they initially believed to be an abandoned SUV off the side of Funny River Road in Soldotna at about five o'clock this evening. Upon investigation, they found the deceased owner inside and are seeking any information or witnesses that might have been in the area this afternoon."

The camera panned again, this time showing a distant shot of a large, white SUV. It reminded me of the SUV that had taxied me around when I first arrived. Police tape had been drawn around the surrounding trees and blue and red lights flashed just off screen. The camera panned back to the reporter. He promised to report more information as it became available then the screen cut into a commercial.

"Weird," Jacey said. "Wonder if the driver had a heart attack or something." She pulled her purse from a locked drawer then powered the TV off.

I wondered if I should call the police and tell them that I'd been in a similar vehicle last night. But, white SUVs were a dime a dozen. If every person who'd seen a similar vehicle called, law enforcement would be inundated. I dismissed the idea almost as fast as it came. It's not like they'd reported a crime scene. They were looking for possible witnesses in the area this afternoon. Like Jacey said, maybe the driver had simply had a heart attack.

Greg propped open the door and poked his head in. "Are you ready to be amazed, young lady?" His smile was brighter than his eyes.

"Can I borrow you for a minute?" Jacey grabbed Greg's arm and pulled him inside before I could answer.

He pinched his brows and shrugged, but followed his sister to the front corner of the store. She showed him the screen of her phone. He whispered something, they nodded in unison, then she whispered something back.

When he turned back toward me, a smile still painted its way across his face. "Adventure awaits, my lady." He hooked his arm into mine and escorted me to the dock.

With each step down the wood planked dock, I reminded myself that there was no better person to keep me safe on a boat than Greg. Rational thoughts, however, did little to calm my irrational anxieties. I chewed at my lip and counted each step until we reached the side of the tin boat. Taking a deep breath, I gripped Greg's hand tightly, then lifted my foot over the edge of the dock and onto shallow boat floor. The boat rocked as I balanced between it and the dock. I waited for the commotion to settle, then lifted my other foot onto the weathered decking.

Greg remained on the dock, an ear to ear grin painted across his face.

"Thank you," he finally said after smiling at me and my subdued panic for several moments.

"For?" I wondered.

"Trusting me enough to get on that boat." He chuckled then offered me his hands. "But I think the other boat will be better for what I'd like to show you."

I twisted my face into a scowl as he helped me step back to the dock. As soon as my feet stabilized I punched him in the arm.

"What was that for?" He gazed down at me with a faux expression of pain.

"You nearly put me into a panic attack over that stupid little tin can and you never intended to take me out on it, did you?"

"I do intend to get you on *that* boat at some point, but not tonight." He slid his hand around my waist and pulled me into him. "The Ooga Booga is much better for night adventures. It has lights and comfortable seating, and"—he winked— "a sound system."

"A sound system, you say?" Not getting lost in his eyes was impossible.

"Yes ma'am." Our bodies pressed together, anchoring my resolve to do whatever might be required to be a part of his life. I hitched my arms around his torso and drew a deep, satisfying breath as he gently pressed his mouth to mine. He claimed to live a dangerous existence, but as our lips danced softly with each other's I felt nothing but a sweet symphony of security.

The warmth of his mouth on mine was a magic salve to my sprinting nerves. Even after parting, the peace of his touch lingered. I climbed on the Ooga Booga with significantly more confidence than I had earlier in the day.

"Wow," I gasped from the boat's deck as I turned toward the horizon. I didn't have words to describe the beauty unfolding in the sky. The customary reds and oranges of sunset faded into vivid strokes of yellows then greens. Bright greens faded to turquoise greens then streaked into a cap of deep blue. The universe itself seemed to be on full display. A blanket of stars like I'd never before witnessed, capped the entire display.

"Oh, you haven't seen anything yet." Greg grinned as he fired up the boat's engine. "The northern lights and a lunar moon are both spectacular on their own, but when you couple them together, the heavens become pure magic." He pointed out the window to the full moon cresting the horizon. "In less than an hour that moon is going to turn a crimson red and all those dancing green lights will pop right out of the sky."

CHAPTER THIRTEEN

Greg wasn't lying when he promised to give me the best seat in the house. As our boat followed the curve of the river first westward, then north, the lights of town disappeared and the heavens lit up with unspeakable beauty. He turned on the sound system and the soft tones of Duke Ellington and his orchestra filled the cabin.

"Lovely," I said, leaning my head into his shoulder as he navigated the boat down river.

"I told you it'd be spectacular." He rested his free arm around me.

"Well, you certainly delivered."

"I try."

"Yes you do," I said, reminded of our dream date to

the symphony in Salt Lake. That'd been our last night together. I sighed at the memory and all the twists and turns that had come our way since then. "Thanks for the flowers. They were lovely."

"What flowers?"

"The one's in my townhome last week. And the one today, on the Jeep."

He throttled back the engine and turned to look at me. "I didn't send you any flowers." He pinched his brows and shook his head. "Who else knows you're here?"

"No one," I shook my head in confusion. If not Greg, then who? And why? An uninvited panic filled my chest. "Maybe David and Todd." I took small comfort in the thought. I'd told David for sure, but not really Todd. I considered the photo of me with my fish. Did it have enough clues to lead them to my specific hotel? And, better yet, had it provided enough information and time for them to send me a flower?

"Hmm." His face contorted as he considered the information. "What kind of flowers?" he asked calmly.

"Lilies, I think. I'm not really a floral expert, but that's what I think they are." My chest began to pound as my mind raced through every possible scenario. There was no way Todd was smart enough to find me, but had David stalked me? If anyone could track me, it'd be him. But would he? And why would he have lied about the lilies in my town home? Or commented that they smelled like a funeral?

"Yes, lilies." A deep, brusque voice sounded behind us.

Greg's arm flew off my shoulder and down to his hip as he quickly snapped around. Surprised by our unexpected guest, I followed suit.

"White stargazers to be exact," the shaded man continued as he pushed the bathroom door closed with his foot. His hands were raised chest level, confidently pointing a gun at Greg. "I'm glad you liked them." He stepped closer. "They symbolize death."

The light of the moon cut across his face, casting deep shadows.

"Ah, Markis, how good to see you." Greg nodded familiarly at the man. His right hand still lay at his hip, ready to snap his weapon at any given moment, but his voice was calm.

My hands trembled and a lump grew in my throat as the two men stared at each other though the darkness. My heard pounded fiercely—I could hear it as definitively as I could feel it raging through my chest and out to my limbs.

"Thanks for all your help, sweetheart." The stranger waved his gun at me. My torso tightened and my body froze. "I probably should feel bad that you are a part of this, but"—his mouth scowled into a tight line— "I don't."

Greg took a step forward and used his left hand to nudge me behind him. "You had your chance to take her out in Utah," Greg said as he placed himself between me and the stranger. "I didn't let you do it then, and I'm most certainly not going to let you now."

Memories of the night Greg kidnapped me from my Utah condo flashed in my memory. *This* was the man Rushton had sent to kill me? *This* was the man Greg had saved me from? The trembling in my hands spread to the rest of my body as sudden recognition hit. I'd seen this man before. Not in Utah, but in Maryland. Those heavy brows and dark, penetrating eyes were hard to forget. Though he hadn't looked like a monster when I confronted him for parking in front of my townhome, he certainly looked the part now. His car had shielded his chiseled physique then, but now, it was apparent. And frightening.

"Yeah, thanks for keeping her alive," he said. The more the man talked, the less polished his English became. I had no knowledge of world languages, but his accent was something I'd certainly never heard before. "She has served her purpose well. Though, I've got to admit, she's a tricky one." He raised his brows and looked beyond Greg's shoulders until his heavy set eyes caught mine. "Sending that cabby to the wrong location to throw me off your tracks? Well-played."

"George?" I whispered.

"Ah, you remember his name. So tender. Don't worry, he didn't rat you out. Nope." He shook his head. "He denied having ever met you right up until the moment I slit his throat."

If someone had kicked me in the ribs, it would've

been more pleasant. "George," I whispered again as the reality of his words hit. The news cast, the police lights, the call for tips. It was all for George. I'd killed George. My fault. Innocent. Man. Dead.

Nausea overtook me. Combatting the sudden urge to puke, I held my breath. "If you wanted to kill me," I asked through trembling lips, "why didn't you just do it in Maryland?"

"Oh, how very naïve you are. And all this time I thought you were a smart one." He shook his head and chuckled. "You're not the catch here. He is." He reaffirmed his gun on Greg's chest. "As soon as your trusty boyfriend double-crossed *The Administrator* and ignored the call for your blood, he became the target." His hedonistic laugh was like a second kick to the gut. "You, my dear, were simply the most delicious bait I've ever employed."

Anger, frustration, and fear boiled within me as the realization of my stupidity hit. I'd been so set on finding Greg, I'd never stopped to consider that someone else might be looking for him, too. I'd been both the hunter and the hunted. And, with his gun positioned confidently at Greg, it was clear that my naivety had come with a very high price tag.

"Do with me what you will, but let the girl go," Greg demanded with a confidence that suggested that I was the only one in panic mode.

"You and I both know that can't ever happen." The man stood firm. "The first rule of making someone disappear is to never leave a witness, isn't that right, Mr. Knight?"

"Clearly you failed on that this afternoon with the cabby. No witnesses, no bodies."

The man shrugged. "Sometimes I like to create a diversion. They're so busy investigating him, they won't even notice that the two of you are gone."

My body trembled from my core to the tips of my limbs. It seemed I'd come all this way only to die in the same deep, watery grave I'd spent my whole life avoiding. How ironic. The sea could've swallowed me years ago in its fury, but tonight it was the rage on board and not the wrath beneath that would be my demise.

I was so busy calculating the probability of getting out alive that I wasn't prepared for Greg to swing into action. With a grace that surely came from his training, he stretched forward in a rapid, smooth movement and kicked the gun out of the man's hand. In swift succession, Greg's body slammed into the man, throwing the both of them to the floor. The dislodged gun spun across the wood decking. The stranger hooked Greg across the jaw with his elbow and Greg's head whipped to the side. He retaliated with a right hook to the man's cheekbone.

I staggered backward, feeling useless in their struggle. My backside hit the boat's control panel, knocking the throttle into a low gear. The boat thrust forward, jolting the fighting men and the unclaimed gun across the deck. Taking note of where the gun settled, I grabbed the throttle stick and pulled it back to a neutral position, then dove across the floor hoping to grab the gun.

My fingers touched the cold, dark composite of the firearm, but before I could tighten my grip on it, the stranger's fist pounded against my cheek. My head jolted to the side, cranking my neck fiercely. I felt my face slap against the ground but the impact was overshadowed by the splitting pain where his fist had crushed into me.

I pulled my knees to my chest, curling against the pain in my head. My eye felt huge, then small. Wet, then dry. The entire left side of my face was throbbing. The cabin was spinning. I closed my eyes to subdue the dizziness then, reminding myself that this was no time to wimp out, forced them open again.

Sure the man had grabbed the gun after hitting me, I was surprised not to see it in his hand. Willing myself to my knees, I watched the two men scuffle out of the corner of my good eye while trying, at the same time, to locate the weapon.

Under the cloak of the night sky—and with only one functioning eye—I could hear and feel each blow with more clarity then I could see them. They were an equal match in strength and training. Every punch Greg threw was met by one from the stranger.

The stranger raised a hard knee into Greg's torso sending a loud thud through the cabin. Greg buckled into the man's body, grabbed hold of his leg, and flipped him to the ground. The man quickly regained his footing, mumbled something in his native tongue, then charged at Greg, pushing them both out the door.

On the outer deck, the two continued their fight. The man cocked his fist back and rushed into Greg. I winced as he delivered one blow, then another. Greg returned the blasts, first to the man's gut then to his face. I wanted to help—wanted to be more than an observer to the nightmare unfolding before me—but I was of no value. My only physical strength was running. That certainly wasn't an asset now. Not to me, and definitely not to Greg.

Reconciled to what I could and couldn't do, I crawled quietly toward the cabin door and scanned the deck for any sign of the missing gun.

Greg grabbed the man's neck and, dropping to his knee pulled his head into his chest. The man's body flipped over Greg's like a rag doll and hit the deck with such force I thought the deck had cracked.

The boat rocked jerkily from one side to the other in direct correlation to the commotion. The sway, combined with the throbbing pain in my face, made my head spin. I crawled to the bench seat just outside the cabin and—intending to use it as leverage to help me stand—rested my aching head on it.

I heard the snap as Greg twisted the man's arm behind his back and pushed him to the ground. I turned in time to see the gun fall from the man's limp fingers, his broken bone protruding disjointedly beneath the fabric of his jacket. Greg picked the gun up and pressed it between the man's eyes.

"Do you think The Administrator will mourn your loss?" Greg held the gun firmly to the man's forehead. The man simply stared at him, his chest heaving in a dramatic rises and falls. "Yeah," Greg answered for him, "I don't think so, either." He pulled the trigger back to its first stop, then held the position in calculable silence as the two stared at each other. "Lucky for you," Greg finally spoke, "I have a policy against using a gun in front of a woman." He relaxed his finger on the trigger, dropped the ammo cartridge to the ground, then tossed the empty gun into the river.

Eyeing the weapon still tucked under Greg's waistband, I considered what it would take to get it in my hands. He may have had a policy, but I didn't.

"Well, that's a stupid policy." The man, stealing his words from my thoughts, thrust himself upward, lunging his good arm toward Greg. By the time I noticed the blade in his hand, he'd smashed it into the flesh at the cusp of Greg's shoulder.

Greg gasped with pain then responded with a kick to the man's abdomen and then another to his face. Blood spurted from the wound as Greg pulled the other man to his feet. His hand tightly grasped at the man's neck. He grumbled something I couldn't quite hear, then pushed the man up into the boat's railing.

The man thrust his knife into Greg's thigh, lodging it deep into the tissue while slamming his head into Greg's. Greg staggered, losing control over the situation long enough for the stranger to turn them both around. Broken arm dangling to his side, the man left his knife in Greg's leg and, sliding his hand up to Greg's throat, pushed him into the railing until his back was buckled helplessly over the edge.

Fueled by an urgency I could only quantify as unequivocal love for Greg, I gripped the edge of the bench seat with both hands and forced myself to stand. The boat rocked and swayed with a fierceness that only magnified the spinning in my head, but that didn't stop my progression. I grabbed the harpoon from its hook beside me and, without thought or premeditation or even a plan, pressed it into the stranger's side and pulled the trigger.

The man went limp, falling forward into Greg. The momentum and weight thrust Greg's precariously balanced torso to bob over the edge of the railing. He reached for the metal rail but couldn't hold the weight of both of their bodies with his wounded arm.

Two bodies—bloodied, broken, and exhausted—tumbled overboard with a splash. The harpoon, still attached to the stranger's side, went with them.

Chapter Fourteen

I rushed to the edge of the boat. Gripping the rail, I scanned the water for any sign of life. The river's current had already washed away the ripples from their fall. I scanned left then right again, but it was hopeless.

I ran into the cabin, flipping every switch on the panel until the boat was lit up like Christmas morning, then ran to the back of the boat in hopes of finding some sign of Greg upstream. Nothing. Not a ripple or a splash, just the peaceful movement of the Kenai.

My chest tightened and I struggled to draw a breath. I'd come so far to find love and just when I thought I had, I'd lost him. Not to pain or heartache or another woman, but to my own stupidity. I'd led a monster to him. I'd brought him right to the front door.

I ran to the front deck then to the back again, skimming my eyes across the water in pure desperation as the boat slowly drifted down stream. Still nothing. I did it again and then again for a third time. "Greg!" I called over and over again into the empty water. "Greg!"

Suffocating in desperation and grief, I gasped and collapsed to the deck. Tears welled heavily in my eyes. I'd lost him. Forever. Me. My fault. Forever.

I drew my knees into my chest and hugged them tightly as I looked up to the sky. The same green lights that had painted their way across the heavens when we'd left the dock were still dancing in beautiful rhythm with the universe. During our skirmish, however, the moon had risen off the horizon and was now burning the brightest red I'd ever imagined. This must've been what Greg had been so excited about. The crimson glow of the lunar moon lay over the neon greens of the northern lights with such glory it was hard not to take notice. It was spectacular. And heavy. Greg had wanted me to see the blood moon and now I'd seen it. And his blood. And the stranger's.

I jumped to my feet and ran to the edge of the boat, barely making it before the contents of my stomach spilled into the water.

My fingers wrapped tightly around the railing as I continued to lean over it. The river bobbed and flowed against the edge of the boat, splashing into the fiberglass and sending a mist up to my face. I closed my eyes and let the frigid spray softly touch my cheeks until they became numb. Numb felt good. Numb felt right.

"Samantha." The call was so soft I was sure I imagined it. I drew a deep breath, holding it while I counted to ten, then released it again. "Samantha." I heard again, this time with a little more vibrato.

"Greg?" I spun around and ran across the deck toward the back of the boat. He had one arm cinched around the prop, the other hanging limply into the water.

"Can you help me, Sam?" he said through labored breath. Water ran off his hair, steaking across his face before making tiny splashes back into the river. "I can barely move my left arm and without it I don't have quite enough strength to climb up over that edge."

"Yes!" Of course, yes! I spun around in search of something to offer him. The answer lay at my feet, nearly tripping me. I reached down and grabbed the anchor rope. "How about a rope?" I called over the edge of the boat.

"Great."

I dropped the rope into the water beside him. Still hanging on to the prop, he swung his injured arm away from his body and grabbed the rope in his fist. He pinched his eyes and grunted softly, then tossed it into his good hand.

There is human strength and then there is sheer human will power. I believe I saw Greg exhibit the second. With open wounds screaming out from his shoulder and his hip, he scaled the anchor rope out of the water and up over the edge of the boat. He dropped the rope as his legs buckled onto the deck.

I fell to my knees beside him. His breath was labored and his flesh was cold.

"Thank you," he said, pressing his hand into the wound at the top of his leg.

"I think we need to get you to a doctor." I gasped at the large hole in his jeans, unsure of the damage that lay beneath.

"How 'bout we start by getting this boat back to the dock?" His face shone red under the crimson glow of the lunar eclipse. "Are you good to drive?"

I could tell by the way he cringed with each word that it wasn't really a question. My body was trembling from fear, his from cold and shock. "Yes," I answered, though I was highly unsure of my newly acquired ability. "But first we need to get you warm."

He hobbled his way into the cabin then, settling in to a seat near the captain's post, directed me to an overhead bin with extra jackets and a few blankets. I placed two blankets over his shoulders, careful not to overburden his wound, then slid out of my oversized coat, draped it over him for good measure, and situated myself in front of the wheel.

He calmly directed my movements, coaching me through each step of the drive. When I saw the light of the Gone Fishin' cabin, I finally resumed breathing.

"Where's the closest hospital?" I asked as he slid

into the passenger seat of his Jeep.

"No hospital," he said, his lips a worrisome shade of purple. His skin was pale and damp. I couldn't tell if it was from the injuries or from being in the cold water for so long. "Take me to your hotel. I'll call someone from there."

"But wouldn't a hospital be better? I think you might need surgery."

"No hospital," he repeated.

Following his instruction, I drove him to my hotel room. Once inside, he used the phone to call someone.

"I think we need to get you out of those clothes," I said as soon as he hung up the phone.

He raised a pained brow and grinned. "I didn't think you were that kind of girl."

"Stop it." I slugged him in his good arm. "You're an ice cube. We've got to get you warmed up."

"If you say so." Cradling his wounded arm close to his body, he gingerly wrestled the wet fabric of his shirt with his good arm. It clung to him like a magnet, making the act of sliding it off nearly impossible.

"Can I help you?" I asked, feeling helpless in his struggle.

"I thought you'd never ask." He grinned through the pain. "There's a knife in my front pocket. I think the only way out of these clothes is to cut them off."

I stepped to his side and slid my hand into the fold of his front pocket, careful not to tug on the fabric in a way that would disturb his wound. The denim was heavy and wet and bitter cold. Plunging my fingers into the fold, I felt the cold steel of his pocket knife. Clenching it between my fingers, I drew it out.

Lifting the saturated cotton of his shirt, I opened the knife and pushed it carefully against the fabric. Working from the bottom hem to his neckline, I cut the jagged slit with little resistance. I did the same down the sleeve that covered his wound.

I cleared the fabric from his torso and tossed it to the floor. When I looked up to assess the wound, he was grinning. "What?" I asked, wondering how he wasn't a big ball of tears. The wound on his arm was raging red. The sides of the incision were swollen and puckered, yet somehow only a few traces of blood trickled out.

"Nothing." He grinned again. "It's just . . ." He smiled at me as he considered his words. "I'm so sorry, Sam. This night didn't go quite how I planned."

"Well, that's good, because if this is what you had planned, you've got a twisted sense of adventure."

"There may be some truth in that." He fumbled, one-handed, with the button on his jeans, finally releasing it before he spoke again. "Just for the record, I don't make a habit of inviting thugs on dates."

"Good to know."

"How are you holding up? I hope it didn't scare you too much."

"I'm fine." I wasn't sure if that was the truth or a lie, but what else was I supposed to say? I had a soaking wet, frozen, half-naked man, with two severe knife wounds standing in front of me. "The real question," I said, trying to remain calm, "is how are you?"

He folded the fly open, gingerly pulling the top of his jeans off of his hip wound, then touched the gaping injury with his fingertips while I tried not to gag. This one was far worse than his arm. The knife had not just penetrated his skin, it'd been twisted in the wound. Ground tissue oozed out the opening.

"This?" he offered a grimaced smile. "Merely a flesh wound."

"I hope so," I whispered. The words were more for myself than for him. What if it wasn't just flesh? What if he'd damaged a major organ? My lip started to quake. What if the hypothermia got him? "Do you want me to cut your pants off, too?" I asked withed feigned confidence. "Or did you want to try to shimmy out of them?"

"I don't think there's going to be a whole lot of shimmying going on from me for a while." The words trickled past his purple lips with a grin.

I shook my head at his inability to take the situation seriously. Maybe he wasn't hurting as much as it appeared he should be. Or maybe the shock had gotten to him.

I instructed him to sit down on the edge of the bed then drew the blankets down and wrapped them around his shoulders. Falling to my knees on the dirty carpet, I wiped the tear from my eye before Greg had a chance to see it, then pulled the knife up the cuff of his jeans. By the time I reached the top, my hands were shaking.

"I didn't expect that the night would end with me getting naked in your room."

"You and me both." I grinned at his sense of humor, hoping that if he felt good enough to make jokes, he also felt good enough to walk away from his injuries. I gently peeled the wet denim away from his injured leg then pulled the heavy, wet remains down his good leg.

"What about these?" He pointed to the boxers still clinging to his body. The wound sat just above them, clearly visible. But the boxers were bloody and soaking wet. I stilled my trembling hand and made a quick cut to free them.

"When is your doctor guy going to be here?" I quickly covered Greg's frozen body with all the hotel blankets in the room. He might have been able to make light of the situation but my stomach was in knots. I needed to know that he was going to be okay. I could've lost him out on that water.

And—I considered the wounds, the chill, and the trauma—there was still a high probability that I could lose him in this room.

"Soon," he said. He closed his eyes and gently lay back into the pillows.

Holding back my tears, I paced the floor, counting the minutes until the doctor arrived. When his knock finally sounded, my heart leapt. I ushered him in then stood back as he examined his patient.

"Ninety-six degrees Fahrenheit." The doctor slipped his thermometer back into his bag. "Not as high as I'd like to see, but not worrisome either. I'm assuming it was significantly lower than that before you got out of those wet clothes."

"You can thank Sam for that." Greg's face was pale and tired as he grinned at me. "She couldn't wait to get me undressed." He winked.

"Well, good job, young lady. You very well could've saved his life."

"I very well could've been the reason he lost his life, too," I mumbled. "Without me he would have never ended up in that water." Moisture fogged up my eyes. I chewed on my lower lip hoping not to break into sobs.

The doctor folded back Greg's blankets and examined the wounds. "It's probably a good thing you went for a swim." The doctor talked to Greg as if I wasn't there. "If the cold water hadn't constricted your veins, you probably would have bled out."

"Looks like all those swimming lessons finally came in handy." Greg closed his eyes as the doctor poked a long needle into several places around the wound just above his hip.

I turned my back and stared at the wall, unable to stomach the makeshift surgery taking place on my hotel bed.

"Sam," Greg's voice cut softly through the silence. "I really am sorry. I should have never put you in this situation."

"What are you talking about?" I turned to face him. "You didn't do this, I did. I led that monster right to you. I was stupid. This is all my fault." The tears I'd been holding back pushed past my heavy lids and rolled down my cheeks. My own wound, though not anywhere near the same league as Greg's, burned with each drop of moisture.

"No it's not." He wiggled his uninjured hand out of the blanket burrito and beckoned for me to come to him. I walked to the opposite side of the bed then, assuring not to disturb the doctor, gently sat down. He wrapped my hand in his. "You are not responsible, Sam. I am. This is part of my job."

"No, Greg. You did everything you could to hide yourself and your family. He'd have never found you without me. I led him right to you. And, what if he's not alone? What if they get to your mom? Or Jacey? Or"— my lip trembled—"Clay?"

He squeezed my hand again. "He didn't, Sam. And they won't. That's all that matters."

I wanted to believe him but I couldn't erase reality. It was my fault.

Holding tightly to his hand, I laid down beside him and rested my head on his shoulder. If I'd have just left things alone, Greg wouldn't be having surgery in a hotel room. He wouldn't have gotten stabbed in the first place or taken a swim in the cold river. And George. George wouldn't be dead.

My body trembled as the tears flowed.

Chapter Fifteen

I'm sure my fellow passengers thought I was going home to a funeral. In a way, I suppose I was. As much as my mind knew that I was a danger to Greg and his family, my heart died more and more with each mile I put between us. I should have never gone to Alaska. I should have never put Greg and his family in jeopardy.

Whatever the doctor had given Greg to help him sleep, had worked like a charm. He was still out like a light when I crawled from his side and packed up my bag. As I kissed his cheek and told him goodbye, I was glad he wasn't conscious enough to register me. Leaving my heart in Alaska was hard enough, doing it to his face would've killed me.

I pressed my face to the airplane window, allowing the cold glass to sooth my swollen cheek and eye. Knowing sleep would likely help me feel better, I willed my mind to shut down. But it couldn't. Every time I closed my eyes, I saw Greg. Or George, my innocent taxi driver. Or the ratty haired man who'd pulled a knife on both of them. The only thing worse than a nightmare, was the horror of real life. I'd had enough death and violence to see me through to eternity.

But it wasn't so much the violence or the fear that drove me away. After hours and hours of sleepless contemplation over the issue, I'd come to the conclusion that I could live with Greg's secret agent status. I could handle never knowing who he worked for and what exactly he did. I could even deal with the time apart as long as he always came home to me. But what I couldn't handle was knowing that *I* wasn't smart enough to keep him safe. *I* was a liability. *I* was the biggest danger in his path. Sure, he'd been okay this time. But what about next time? Or the time after that?

I buried my face in my hands as the tears started again. The businessman in the seat next to me shifted in his seat then, pretending not to notice me, cranked up the volume in his headphones. I didn't blame him. I'd have done the same thing.

Fourteen hours and two layovers later, my plane touched down on Maryland soil. The sun crested the eastern horizon, welcoming another day. A new day. The first in a lifetime of days that I'd have to live without the biggest piece of my heart. As I tossed my backpack onto the passenger seat of my car, I tried to convince myself that I'd be okay. Time would heal my wounds just as assuredly as they'd heal Greg's and we'd both move on with life as if nothing ever happened.

The clock on my dash read 5:54 a.m. as I entered the freeway. I made a mental checklist of the things I needed to accomplish before reporting to work at 9:00 am. It consisted of three items: get home, take a shower, try to sleep. The first two were doable, the second would likely be fruitless for days.

As I pulled into my garage, my stomach growled

with a ferocity that reminded me that I hadn't eaten a real meal for a long time. I pushed the thought aside and slid the transmission into park then added 'eat' to my mental to-do list.

Grabbing my backpack off the passenger seat, I stepped out of the car and slung it over my shoulder with the last drop of energy I had. With a sigh, I shuffled my heavy feet through the garage and unlocked my townhome door.

I stepped inside and immediately turned back to relock the deadbolt. I managed to snap the door closed before my heart stalled and my breathing stopped.

"Once you've entrusted your secrets to a stranger, they can never be a stranger again." The voice hit my back, but it was as familiar as my own hand. I didn't need to see his face to know who it was. But I wanted to see his face. Ached to. But I froze.

My keys slid from my hand and hit the floor. "Greg?" I breathed his name as if I'd heard a ghost.

My heart picked up speed as I slowly spun around. Greg leaned against my kitchen counter, one arm in a sling, the other holding a cane. He'd traded the scruffy beard and jeans from the day before for a tailored suit and clean shaven cheeks. "Hi, Sam," he smiled. His lip was swollen and his face shone in various shades of red, blue, and purples.

"But, how?" Everything in me wanted to run to him and take him in my arms. My feet, however, anchored themselves firmly to the floor by the door.

"Private jets don't have layovers." His eyes winced as he shrugged his shoulders.

"Why are you here?" I asked, unsure how to categorize his presence. My emotions were in the throes of an inward battle. I loved him with all that I had but my weekend rendezvous had proven that we couldn't be together. "You shouldn't be here." My lip trembled.

"And where should I be?"

"In a hospital bed," I started my thought, not intending the second half to come out of my mouth. It, however had different plans. "Far away, where I don't have to look at you." A tear dropped from my eye and rolled down my cheek.

He shook his head. "I don't think you mean that." He readjusted himself against the counter, trying to keep the weight off his left leg. Though covered by his clothing, the bulk of his bandage was hard to miss.

"This thing can't work. I almost got you killed."

"Not true." He took a hobbled step toward me, securing his weight with my counter top.

"Absolutely true," my voice shook. "I'm terrible at secrets."

"Also not true. I've seen what you can do with a computer." He gingerly lifted his injured leg and took another limped step toward me.

"Virtual secrets are a completely different game than real world ones. I just don't think I'm cut out for the world you live in." Another tear touched my cheek as I calculated the events that led to his swollen, hammered face. I shifted my eyes to the floor. "Eventually," I stammered at the thought, "I'll get you killed."

"To be fair, you didn't know what you were up against." His voice moved closer.

"And I still don't. Not really." And I never would. His employment ensured that.

He lifted his right leg, then secured his cane to the

floor before dragging his left one forward. "We can change that," he said. His movement came to a stop directly in front of me. He touched his hand to my chin and gently raised it.

I stared at him "Stop," I said, my damp eyes glaring into his. "Stop making promises you can't keep."

"I don't make promises I can't keep, Sam."

My lip trembled. I wanted—more than anything I'd ever wanted before—to believe him.

His hand gently glided under my jaw then he moved his thumb over my cheek. Softly wiping my tears, he said, "I have someone I need you to meet." With a tender push of his hand, he turned my head toward the living room.

Realizing that we weren't alone, I blushed. I'd been so caught up with the man in my kitchen I'd completely missed the two in my living room. "David?" I asked, baffled by the presence of both men, but especially him.

"Hi. Sa. Man. Tha," he nervously stuttered my name in broken syllables from his position on the couch.

"It's about time," the tall bald man interrupted. "I was just about to puke at the love fest." With square shoulders, he stood confident in his generic black suit and bland black tie. His arms crossed assertively behind his back, his feet stacked directly under his shoulders. "Please come sit next to Mr. Carey. What I have to say applies to the both of you." His chiseled jaw squared with each word, conveying an authority I didn't dare refute.

I glanced at David, then at the man, then back at Greg. Greg swiped his thumb across my cheek again, then nodded his affirmation and stepped out of my way.

I felt like a guest in my own house as I slowly left Greg behind me and moved across the floor. Apprehensively, I dropped my backpack to the floor and slid onto the sofa beside David. My hands knotted into each other and fell onto my lap. I looked over and noticed that David's hands had done the same thing.

"I'm General Casey." The man offered a single nod then paced to my right. "I've been watching the two of you."

My chest tightened at what I felt was an accusation.

His face remained hard and unrevealing as he continued. "You permeated the government's darkest networks and purged even the most hidden of data. Technically, you broke the law to do it."

I swallowed hard then glanced up at Greg. He'd pitched himself against the counter again, taking the weight off his leg.

The general's gate halted and he turned himself square to David. "Mr. Carey," he nodded at David. David's hands massaged over each other nervously and I heard him swallow. The general then turned to me. "Miss Perry." Another nod. I tucked my hands under the side of my thighs and held my breath. "The two of you have proven to be quite the team. You've gotten through firewalls and deciphered data the government had gone through a great deal of trouble to hide." He paced three steps to the left, halted, then paced back in front of us before stopping again. "You've proven to be competent allies to the cause for peace and freedom. We want you on our team."

David and I looked at each other.

"I'm sorry," I finally said, looking from Greg to the general and back again. "I don't understand."

General Casey answered. "We've been working to

STEPHANIE CONNELLEY WORLTON

shut down an Armenian crime ring in the U.S. Their game is fraud. Credit card skimming, gas theft, and ultimately identity manipulation. Their networks are deep and their pockets are even deeper."

"Is this somehow connected to Peter Rushton?" I wondered.

"Yes. But Rushton was just a middle man. They paid him for his expertise knowing greed would get the best of him. They counted on him to crack before they made a complete pay out, and they were right. They are very good at what they do." He raised his brows as he looked at me then at David. "And clearly, so are the two of you. We need your skill set to track them down and take them out. We need you on our team."

I measured each breath as I considered his words.

David pushed his glasses up higher on his nose and looked up at the general. "I'm not sure what you're asking."

Greg stabbed his cane onto the floor and slowly maneuvered his way across the room. "He's offering you a contract. We need you and Sam on our team."

"We can't give you the specifics until you sign."

General Casey puffed his chest. "But you should know it would require some sacrifice. You'd be moved to a secure location, given a new identity, and have restricted contact with your family. You'd also receive tactical training—not enough to be the strategic asset Knight is, but enough to keep yourselves and your team members alive if your situation were to become compromised."

"Do I have a choice?" David fidgeted.

"Of course. Everyone always has a choice," General Casey affirmed. "I, for example, could *choose*"—he stressed the word— "to hand my findings over to the NSA. I can't say for certain what they would *choose* to do with that information, but it's fair to assume that the possibility you'd be out of a job is a real one."

"Blackmail." David leaned forward and ran his hands over his balding head.

"Diplomacy," the general corrected. "As soon as we shut down the Armenians your contract would expire."

David's mouth turned down. "And how long do you perceive that being?" He looked like he might pass out.

"Months." The general shrugged. "Or years. Hard

to say."

I considered the options, feeling bad for the situation I'd put David in, but ultimately only caring about one thing.

Greg supported himself on the back of a chair. I could tell he was in pain, but he didn't complain. "Would we be together?" I asked.

Greg looked over at the general, held his gaze for a few moments, then nodded. "Yes," he turned to me with a grin. "You wouldn't necessarily come out on every assignment, but we'd be stationed at the same headquarters. We'd be a team."

"A team?" I repeated the words. They sounded almost too good to be true.

"Yes." Greg nodded.

"Does this mean I'm headed to Alaska?"

"No," General Casey answered. "The security of the mission has been compromised in Alaska. Knight and his family will have to be relocated until the area can be re-secured." He didn't make a complete accusation, but I felt the sting of his words.

"I'm sorry," I looked into Greg's eyes. "I know how

much you love Alaska."

"Not as much as I love you."

General Casey cussed. "At least have the curtesy to let me leave the room before you open up on all the PDA junk." He let out a grunted sigh and offered Greg and me the death stare. "Don't make me regret the decision to let you work together. I'm not a fan of fraternization on my team."

I waited for the general and David to excuse themselves before throwing my arms around Greg. "Are you sure you want me on your team?" I was genuinely worried that he hadn't thought through all the ramifications of such an offer. "I mean, seriously. Look at you."

"I'd rather look at you."

"Stop." I nudged his good shoulder with my palm.

"I can't."

"But I'm such a liability. And"—I touched my bruised face— "a pansy."

"And that's why we'll keep you in an office. Last time I checked, computers don't throw punches." He slid his hand up the base of my neck and pressed his lips to mine.

"No more secrets," I said when I finally came up for air.

"No more secrets." He winked. "At least from each other."

Epilogue

"I'm not sure what's going on there." Greg settled into the patio chair beside me. His arm had healed almost completely, but his leg still moved gingerly by the end of each day.

"I think it's pretty obvious." I rested my hand on his knee and stared out across the sand. Greg's injuries had hampered his work load, but I didn't mind. Recovery time meant that he was grounded, on sabbatical, nursing his wounds until he was strong enough to handle the physical demands of his assignment. Nearly two months of hiding in plain sight on the warm beaches of the Florida Keys had left the both of us sun-kissed and smiling.

Leaning toward me, Greg pushed a wayward hair

off my face and, smiling at the blonde curls that refused to be tamed, graced me with a kiss. I'd never been a blonde before, but after eight weeks of my new bottled color, I'd grown to like it. The sun, the sand, and the man by my side all seemed to be a good fit.

"Look at her." Greg smiled at his sister as she kicked her bare feet across the sand. Her jeans were rolled up in thick folds baring her calves. She smiled brightly as she watched Clay play in the surf. "I should've taken her out of Alaska a long time ago."

General Casey had set us up with a beach rental—a three-bedroom bungalow in the heart of a tourist area where nobody questioned the comings and goings of the seasonal occupants. Occupants meaning us. And by us, I mean John and Susanne Winters. Not Greg or Seth or Sam or Ginger. John and Susanne. Married, just for show for the moment, but with each passing day I looked forward to the time we could make the ring on my finger a permanent one.

Kristen, Jacey, and Clay shared the remaining bedrooms of the rental. General Casey called them "collateral damage" and insisted that the clean-up in Alaska was moving along swiftly so they could return home. I'm not entirely sure that Jacey was in a hurry.

"I don't think it's the beach that's making her happy," I said.

For Greg's family, the stint in the Keys was like an extended, government funded vacation. For the rest of, however, it was work. David and I reported every morning for four hours of tactical training, martial arts intensives, and physical tortures I never imagined possible. When we finished getting our butt's kicked, we spent the rest of the day in the detached garage on my and Greg's rental property. The entire two-car space had been converted into our computer lab and team headquarters.

And it was torturous work. Hacking and digging and hacking some more. Five other members of our now ten-person team—including David, our individual trainers, another computer geek, and General Casey—had condos within five minutes of us. The other three were nameless shadows located in covert places. I knew the time would come when that could be my reality—and in a sense, it already had—but I had Greg and that's all that mattered to me.

"If it's not the beach"—Greg laced his fingers through mine— "what do you suppose it is?"

I slid my sunglasses to the top of my head as if that would help me better evaluate the situation. David's hibiscus print shirt was buttoned down a few notches, revealing a chest almost as hairless as his head. It'd taken him some time to trade his khaki pants and boring collared shirts for a more relaxed wardrobe, but with time and a little coaching, he'd adapted to his new environment. Or, as the blue and gold floral print of his shirt testified, maybe over adapted.

He stood, stiff-legged in the sand, making disjointed movements with his hands that I'm sure mimicked the stuttered words that were slipping out of his mouth. Whatever it was, must've been funny. Either that or so ridiculous Jacey had no choice but to laugh. She tucked her hands in her jean pockets and, lifting her head energetically, tossed her ponytail over her shoulder.

"You don't think . . .?" Greg leaned back in his chair and twisted his ball cap so it was backward. Neither one of us could finish the thought, but we were both thinking it.

I twisted in my chair, very aware of the new firearm concealed just below my bust line. "Stranger things have happened." I shrugged then, leaning over, pressed my lips to Greg's.

*** THE END ***

Thank you for reading HUNTED, The Final HACK and the rest of The SECRET OF SECRET SERIES. I hope you enjoyed Samantha's story as much as I enjoyed writing it. I love hearing what my fans have to say. If you enjoyed what you just read, please take a minute to leave a review on **Amazon**, Goodreads, or any other media outlets you use.

If you liked The SECRET OF SECRET SERIES *(aka: The HACKED Series)*, you might also enjoy my novel, *All the Finer Things.*

Megan Hamilton's posh life, designer clothes, and stunning penthouse leave her wanting for nothing . . . or do they? Controlled by his obsessive pursuit of perfection, Doctor Matthew Hamilton will stop nothing short of breaking his young, spirited bride into a subservient trophy wife. How far will Megan have to go to escape Matt's obsessive control and abuse? And how much will she have to lose before she gets there?

Please enjoy the first chapter:

All the Finer Things

A Novel ~

- Sometimes money costs too much.

Chapter One

The front door closed almost as abruptly as it opened, rattling the framed photos on the wall. A rippling chill coursed through the dark foyer and into the parlor at the clank of car keys tossed onto the glass entry table. There was a brief, hopeful moment of silence before the hard soles of Matt's patent leather shoes thumped their way heavily over the polished mahogany floor. Megan sat motionless on the low-backed sofa, watching his labored movement across the obsessively organized room. Pursing her lips so tightly they'd become numb, she waited for his recognition.

"What are you still doing up?" He pulled his already loosened tie off his neck and tossed it - along with his suit coat - over the back of a sleek-lined black leather chair.

Wrapping her fingers around a brightly hued throw pillow, Megan swallowed back the anger threatening to burst out of her. "I was waiting for you." The words slid out across her quivering lips.

Shrugging off her comment, Matt worked his fingers down the front of his tailored dress-shirt, fumbling with each button as he did so.

Megan positioned the pillow intently into its place on the sofa before she stood. "I..." she curled her toes into the white shag throw rug, clenching back her frustration as she rephrased her thought. "Next time you're going to be late, can I please get a phone call?" She thought it was a reasonable request, considering, he expected to have dinner on the table precisely at seven o'clock.

Her bare feet left the plush warmth of the throw rug and padded their way across the cold wood floor towards the dining room. She gathered his unused utensils from the head of the glass dining table and placed them on top of his untouched, now five-hour-cold, chicken parmesan.

"Sorry," he said, non-apologetically, giving up on the third button. "I had some stuff to do at the office."

"I'll bet," Megan mumbled to herself. She gathered his dishes into her hands and, stopping just long enough to blow out the flickering stub of a candle on the center of the table, paced heavily into the kitchen.

Guided only by the illumination of the city lights pressing through the floor-to-ceiling windows, her feet made the distinction between the smooth finish of the hardwood that interlaced most of their two-bedroom penthouse and the rough, unforgiving texture of the eighteen inch slate on the kitchen floor. Making her way around the sizable island, she dumped Matt's warm drink into the sink. Focused on controlling her frustration, she pulled at the lip on the cabinet face, opening a well-disguised trash compactor.

"You got something you want to talk about?" Matt's voice echoed from the doorway.

Flinching at his tone, she dumped his dinner – plate and all - into the trash. "No," she offered softly, hoping to diffuse her husband's flippancy. The gate of his long-legged stance and the shiftiness of his tilted stagger were indication enough that he'd had more than a few drinks. Now was not the time to pick a fight.

Reaching her hand into the trash she retrieved the dropped plate. The cold slime of pasta and tomato sauce slopped over her skin and under her manicured nails causing her to cringe.

"Do you think ignoring me will solve your problem?"

Her problem. It was always *her* problem.

He didn't wait for an answer. "This is absolutely ridiculous – you stomping around this house like you're so hard done by. I give you everything…" he swung his arms out from his torso indicating the exquisiteness of their home and pricey possessions. "And just because I'm a little late coming home you think you have the right to get all huffy?"

Huffy? She set the tomato coated plate into the sink basin then stuck her hands under the tap, allowing the warm water to rinse over them. "I'm not huffy," she smiled over her shoulder, hoping he wouldn't catch the quiver in her voice or, worse yet, read unintentional indignation into it.

He moved across the room in three easy steps. "Then what are you?" He pressed his chest against her shoulders. His hot breath stung at her neck.

"I…" she shrugged. "I'm just tired and…" She didn't want to finish the thought. She didn't want to make him mad. She couldn't tell him that he'd hurt her. Today, of all days, he'd forgotten her. Surely he'd jotted the date down at least once while at the office. *Had he failed to make the connection or did he simply not care?* She shut the water off then wrapped her hands into a dishtowel.

"And what?" he grabbed her arms roughly, spinning her around to face him. His eyes, like weather worn battleships, were hard and grey. She'd already triggered something – a trace of the rage within him. "And what?" he demanded again.

Megan had to force herself to swallow. She had to stay calm. "And… and I was worried." Her heart was racing. She forced another smile. "I left a half a dozen messages on your cell phone," she explained, "and when you didn't call back… I… I started to get worried."

"Well here I am," he spat the words at her, "safe and sound like the big boy that I am!"

She flinched at the pungency of alcohol that lurched through Matt's lips and into her face. "What?" He gripped her arm even tighter, cocking his head as the last hint of softness drained from his face. "Am I not allowed to have a little drink after a hard day at work?"

She blinked back the fear in her eyes, afraid to speak. Afraid to cry.

"Huh?" he yelled, unnecessarily loud. "Answer me woman!"

"No, Matt… you know it's not like that," she tried to wiggle her arms free of his hurtful grasp, but that only made him constrict his fists tighter. "I'm sorry you had a bad day," a tear dropped down her cheek. Despite her sincerity, his demeanor held as tightly as his hands. The dishtowel fell limply to the floor.

"Did you make it to the gym today?" His glare was so intense she considered lying just to make him happy. He raised his eyebrows – an invitation to cross him.

"No," she dropped her head dejectedly. "Jacob was running a fever so I thought it'd be better for me to stay with him." She hoped he'd appreciate her truth but doubted the existence of any tender mercy. Even before she'd given birth to their son, Matt's disgust with her had begun to boil into fury. In the ten short months of Jake's life, Matt's discontent had become outright terrifying.

Every perfectly sculpted muscle in his face

contorted as he tightened his jaw. "Why can't you understand that I have an image to maintain? I have one of the most successful practices in the city. Do you think that comes without a price?" He lashed out and in a sudden movement her body flew across the room. Her hands, still tingling with the numbness from his grip, smacked onto the slate floor, cushioning the blow to her knees. Her forehead, however, was spared nothing as it struck the refrigerator door. Anchoring herself for another blow, she rolled into a ball and closed her eyes against the blurring spots in her vision.

"I should've never agreed to let you have *that baby*! I should've known that you'd be too lazy to take care of yourself." He shook his head. "Look at you. You're disgusting! The last thing a plastic surgeon can afford is a fat wife!"

What about a mangled one? The irony of his accusation seemed lost in the fire of his rage. Megan swiped at the warm stream on her forehead, preventing the trickle of blood from reaching her eye.

"I only weigh three pounds more than I did before I had him," she whispered. She thought of their sleeping son down the hallway as she gripped the edge of the countertop and pulled herself to her feet. Three pounds seemed like a small price to pay for such a sweet angel.

"Three pounds? Are you sure that's all?" Matt lunged at her, gripping the soft skin under her belly button. "Maybe I need to schedule a little nip-tuck for you. This…" he pinched roughly, leaving the indents of his fingertips in a bruise, "is unacceptable."

"Is that why you're having an affair?" As soon as the words slipped over her lips she wished she could suck them back in. This wasn't the time to bring up his new twenty-year old, bleach blonde, legs-to-the-moon receptionist.

"You think I'm having an affair?" He raised his brow over fury blazon eyes. "I have dinner with one of my assistants and all of a sudden I'm having an affair?" He knotted the neck of her blouse in his fist and twisted it powerfully into the base of her chin. She strained to keep her toes in contact with the tiles as her heels left the floor.

"I thought you said you had a bad day at work, not that you'd been out with Ashlee." Megan fired back before she could stifle the remark. She knew better than to egg him on. *Bite your tongue,* she warned herself. But it was already too late.

The tip of Matt's nose touched hers as he leaned in. "I *did* have a rough day," he barked. "And if I decide to go out to get some drinks or have some dinner, that's none of your business, is it?" It wasn't a question. He lifted her up by the tuft of her shirt and slammed her backwards into the pantry door before releasing his hold. Her bare feet closed the distance to the floor in record time and crashed brutally into the rough tile. A shock thrust from her ankles to her hips. Her knees buckled. Arms flailing, she tried hopelessly to gain control of her falling body. Blindly, she reached for the counter top. Her hand slid across the slick granite, pushing a glass sugar bowl in its path. Her body tumbled helplessly to the floor but not before sugar and glass were scattered from one corner of the kitchen to another.

"Now look what you've done," Matt's voice shook the glasses in the cupboard. "I'd suggest you clean up your mess before you come to bed." He kicked the broken jar out of his way. "I'd hate for Alessandra to have to deal with it in the morning."

He dusted his shoe over the sugar, spreading the pile even further across the floor. Rubbing his hand through his golden locks, he released another intoxicated breath as he squatted down to her level. "Why do you insist on making me so angry, Megan?" His voice was suddenly calm. "I wish you wouldn't push me so far." He tilted her chin up with the tip of his finger, forcing her to look at his smug face as his voice softened even more. "You know how much I hate fighting, and…" he touched the wound on her forehead gently, "I'm really sorry about this." He ran his eyes over the wound, expertly assessing the damage. "It's pretty superficial," he nodded. "Just a tiny little cut. Head wounds are always bleeders but it'll heal pretty fast. You'll be as good as new in couple of days. Just like it never happened." He stood up, slid his hands into the pockets of his slacks and turned to leave.

"Hurry and get this mess cleaned up," he added on his way out the door. "I'm tired." He sauntered out of the room, kicking arrogantly at the sugar dust as he went.

Megan slumped back into the floor, her body shaking uncontrollably. She buried her face into her hands, grateful Matt's anger had dissolved as quickly as it had. She'd lost count of all the times before when it hadn't.

Her head throbbed and swirled with pain. The tops of her arms were throbbing too, pressurizing tighter and tighter with each beat of her heart, as if his hands were still wrapped fiercely around them. Slowly, she gained her composure then crawled away from the pantry door and methodically pulled her way off the floor.

He was right about at least one thing, she admitted: the wounds were just superficial. Her heart, however, had suffered a near fatal blow. "Happy anniversary," she whispered as she reached for the broom. "Happy anniversary, Matt."

Get the rest of the story on Amazon
or at www.StephanieWorlton.com

About the author

Stephanie lives in the shadow of the Rocky Mountains where she enjoys frequent opportunities to observe nature and feed her creative spirit. She has been blessed to be a stay at home mom to her four children, many of whom share her artistic tendencies. In addition to writing, she spends her days designing, building, painting, drawing, landscaping, and snuggling with her dogs. She has her own collection of power tools, a plethora of camera equipment, and a passion for shoes.

Connect with Stephanie online
   Facebook
   www.stephanieworlton.com
   Amazon Author Page
   Goodreads Author Page

OTHER BOOKS BY STEPHANIE:

Hope's Journey - High school seniors, Sydney and Alex think they have life all figured out, until one decision turns their plans upside down. Faced with pending parenthood, they must learn to forgive each other – and themselves – if they have any hope of moving on.

All the Finer Things - Megan Hamilton's posh life, designer clothes, and stunning penthouse leave her wanting for nothing . . . or do they? Controlled by his obsessive pursuit of perfection, Doctor Matthew Hamilton will stop nothing short of breaking his young, spirited bride into a subservient trophy wife. How far will Megan have to go to escape Matt's obsessive control and abuse? And how much will she have to lose before she gets there?